CHRISTMAS SWITCH

CHRISTMAS SWITCH

This Christmas, it's her turn to let go...
and his turn to hold it all together

KATE HENDRICKSON

Christmas Switch
Kate Hendrickson

Bell & Ink Publishing

© 2025 by Kate Hendrickson

This is a work of fiction. Names, characters, businesses, places, events, and incidents are either the product of the author's imagination or used fictiously. Any resemblance to actual persons, living or dead, or actual events is purely coincidental.

ISBN: 979-8-9995955-0-8

Book Coaching by: Anne Brooks/ www.annebrooksauthor.com
Edited by: Bryn Donovan/ www.bryndonovan.com
Cover & Interior Design by: Emma Elzinga/ www.inksplatterdesign.com
Author Headshot: ©Evelyn Laws/ www.evelynlaws.com

For my husband —

who supports all my wild ideas and is somehow even more excited about this book than I am.

You're my biggest cheerleader, my sounding board, and the reason I believed I could do this.

P.S. We are never switching Christmas duties.

Prologue

BEEP. BEEP. BEEP.

As the alarm shrieked, Tommy frantically fanned it with a dish towel. A thin layer of smoke clouded the entire kitchen. As the potatoes boiled over on the stove, he grabbed the pot barehanded, yelping as the scorching metal seared his skin. He jerked it off the burner, splashing steaming water onto his shirt as the pot clattered against the stove. In disbelief, he could only stare at the disaster around him.

Ali stormed into the disastrous scene; "What now?" she shouted, slamming her hands onto the counter.

Tommy glared at his wife. "Oh, so now it's my fault?"

"Yes! All this is your fault!" Ali snapped. "Switching Christmas was your idea, genius!"

"I remember, sweetheart," he bit back. He saw her eyes narrow, she hated when he called her that, and he knew it.

"Where's the dog?" he barked, coughing through the haze.

"We don't have a dog!" she shot back, before her eyes widened in realization. "Lulu!"

At the sound of her name, a slight blur of fur darted past Tommy's legs. Sirens continued to howl from outside, drowning out Lulu's high-pitched bark and red lights flickered through the front windows.

"Perfect," Tommy muttered, wiping soot off his face. "The whole neighborhood gets a front-row seat to this chaos."

"You are not helping," Ali snapped.

Madness swirled around them—the barking dog, the blaring alarm, the scent of ruined dinner hanging in the air. Tommy looked down at the scorched countertop, feeling the weight of everything crashing down.

Tommy turned to Ali, who leaned heavily against the counter, a quiet sadness etched across her face. He had wanted to prove he could manage Christmas, that she didn't have to do it all alone, but somehow it had all gone wrong. Christmas was ruined.

CHAPTER 1

Thanksgiving, Four Weeks Earlier

Ali Crawford glanced around her meticulously arranged kitchen one last time before turning out the lights and heading up the stairs. A sense of contentment washed over her as she made her way through the house. This Thanksgiving had been nothing short of spectacular. The tablescape, adorned with her newly acquired pale orange linens, her grandmother's exquisite Wedgwood china, and the vibrant autumn lilies she had carefully selected from the flower truck could easily grace the glossy pages of a lifestyle magazine. Despite feeling utterly drained after two full days of culinary orchestration and thorough tidying, the joy of lavishing her family with a feast to celebrate the holiday made her hard work worthwhile.

The house was quiet for the first time all day. Her kids had retreated to their rooms about an hour earlier, and she had left her husband, Tommy, asleep on the couch after turning off the Cowboys game. He would make it to the bedroom soon, but this was her chance for a few minutes of solitude. The allure of a leisurely soak in the bath, accompanied by a final glass of Cabernet, tugged at her as she reflected on the day and began to quietly plot for the next grand occasion: Christmas.

The thought of Christmas was exhausting. Every year, she would declare, *"There should be more time between Thanksgiving and Christmas,"* and those thoughts returned now as Thanksgiving came to a close. After indulging in her bath and savoring the rich wine, she slipped into her softest cotton pajamas and laid her head on the pillow. Retrieving her phone, she navigated to the calendar and counted the days. Twenty-nine. *"Twenty-nine days until Christmas,"* she muttered as her husband fell into bed beside her.

"Twenty-nine? We've got time," he said.

Ali shot him a look of annoyance only a wife of eighteen years could give. She loved her husband beyond measure, but sometimes the words she wanted to say, or the looks she gave him, told a different story.

"Twenty-nine days is *not* a lot of time," she began. "I have to pick out all the gifts, wrap every single one of them, coordinate Noah's holiday celebration at school, mail Christmas cards, organize the annual party for our friends, volunteer at church for the Angel Tree, prepare Christmas Eve dinner, Christmas breakfast, and—"

"I get it, I get it," Tommy interrupted, rolling over to bring the conversation to a close. They laid in silence for a few moments, but Tommy couldn't resist. "I put up the Christmas lights *and* the tree so we can decorate it."

Ali shot him another side-eye. "And don't forget decorating. There's so much decorating." With that, she turned over, ready to surrender to sleep. She lacked the energy to prolong the conversation and had no desire to end the day with an argument. They rarely fought and going to bed in the middle of a disagreement was the worst. Before she knew it, Tommy was sound asleep, again. She, on the other hand, would toss and turn most of the night, thinking about her Christmas to-do list.

The following morning, Ali woke up early, though not as early as Noah. Their energetic six-year-old was a firecracker who exploded out of bed every morning by 6:30, eager to take on the day. Roughly a year ago, Ali and Tommy had taught Noah how to switch on cartoons and grab a snack so they could snooze for an extra thirty minutes. Ali peeked into the living room and found him immersed in the Macy's Thanksgiving Parade, which they had recorded the previous day, and Noah had already watched twice. He sat with the entire box of Cheerios in his lap as he nibbled away contentedly.

Ali made her way into the kitchen, turned on the coffee pot, and retrieved a bowl from the cabinet before sliding next to Noah for some cherished morning cuddles. She gently slipped the cereal box out of his hands, poured the Cheerios into the bowl, and giggled with him at the Snoopy float, dancing its way down 6th Avenue.

Tommy joined them about ten minutes later, carrying two steaming cups of coffee, one for himself and one for Ali. Their older children had yet to come downstairs and likely wouldn't for at least another hour.

Pierce, their sixteen-year-old son, had started spending more time secluded in his room, distancing himself from his younger siblings. Even if he were awake, he wouldn't emerge until hunger forced him out. Maddie, their thirteen-year-old daughter, and the only girl, had recently embraced her teenage status by sleeping as late as possible. Ali often had to wake her on weekends, or she might not appear until midday.

Eventually, both teens shuffled into the kitchen, where the family gathered around the table, nibbling on cinnamon rolls. Between bites, Tommy asked, "What should we do today?"

Before anyone else could chime in, Ali answered, "We have to put away the Thanksgiving decorations. If we can accomplish that, we can put up the tree this weekend." It was typical for the Crawford family to devote the weekend after Thanksgiving to decorating the house for Christmas, so Ali's plan didn't catch any of them by surprise.

Following breakfast, the kids lazed around, watching TV and playing video games, while Tommy and Ali tackled cleaning up the breakfast remnants and tidying up around the house. As Ali grabbed her notebook from the kitchen desk, Tommy recognized what was coming—the list.

"I'm heading out to the garage," Tommy muttered as he crept out of the kitchen. Ali glanced in his direction, but her focus was elsewhere. She was determined to make this Christmas the best one yet. Well, not entirely on her own—Tommy helped—but Christmas was her domain.

Christmas Prep

- ☐ *Pack up Thanksgiving decorations*
- ☐ *Buy stamps for Christmas cards*
- ☐ *Dust shelves*
- ☐ *Sweep and mop*
- ☐ *Update December calendar*
- ☐ *Remind Tommy to bring decorations down from the attic to inventory and organize*
- ☐ *Replace lights and ornaments, if needed*

"Pierce, Maddie— I'm running to the post office to grab stamps before the Christmas ones are gone. Can you start cleaning up around the house while I'm out? Pierce, downstairs, and Maddie, you knock out the upstairs." Ali called from the bottom of the stairs, her voice echoing through the hallway as she clutched her purse and keys.

There was a brief pause. Ali heard a TV show humming from the living room, followed by footsteps shuffling above. Then, Maddie's voice rang out from upstairs. "Do we get Mom money for this?"

Ali smirked, knowing exactly what motivated her kids. "Mom money" had become a staple in their household—an incentive system Ali had devised to get through the daily grind of parenting. The currency could be exchanged for real money, trips to the local ice cream shop, or something from the coveted treasure box, a little chest filled with colorful trinkets, candy, and the occasional small toy. While Pierce and Maddie had outgrown the thrill of digging through the treasure box and preferred cold hard cash, Noah still approached it with wide-eyed excitement, gravitating towards matchbox cars and lollipops.

"Yes!" Ali yelled one more time before heading out the front door. She highly doubted much would get done while she was gone, but she figured the promise of Mom money might at least spark a small attempt. Turning the corner toward the garage, she found Tommy in his sanctuary, beer in hand, at his workbench.

"I'm off to the post office. Need anything while I'm out?" she asked, stepping into the garage where the crisp air hit her face. The winter breeze always put her in a festive mood.

Tommy glanced up from the mess of wrenches and wires, raising his beer bottle with a grin. "Got it covered," he replied, giving her a wink. His carefree demeanor never ceased to both amuse and frustrate her.

Ali smirked. "I might stop at the liquor store for myself on my way back. Oh, I asked the kids to clean up a bit."

Tommy chuckled, taking a swig of his beer. They both knew the house would likely look the same when she returned, except for maybe a few toys tossed into the chest in the playroom.

"Good luck with that," Tommy teased.

Ali slipped into her car, grateful for a few minutes of calm. Sometimes, a quick errand run felt like a mini-vacation; a quiet, solitary moment to reset. She switched on the radio, the smooth hum of Nat King Cole's "Chestnuts Roasting on an Open Fire" filling the car as she hummed along.

The post office parking lot was packed; Ali circled the parking lot three times before someone finally backed out. Inside the line was long, snaking back to the entryway, filled with people clutching stacks of holiday cards and packages. Ali entered the queue, glancing around at the holiday decorations, snowflakes hanging from the ceiling, a tiny tree in the corner. She tapped her foot, rehearsing her request in her head. She had her heart set on the festive candy cane stamps she'd spotted online. Every year, she liked to use special ones for her Christmas cards. The candy canes felt whimsical and playful, perfectly suited for the Crawford family's annual card, with a picture that featured the kids in identical sweaters while making silly faces. Before kids, she had favored holiday flower-themed stamps, but now, she liked the more playful ones.

As the line crept forward, Ali occupied herself with people-watching. A man in front of her, juggling two packages and a roll of tape, muttered under his breath as one of his boxes toppled to the floor. Ali grabbed it for him to make sure he didn't tumble over with it. Behind her, an older woman was gossiping animatedly with a friend about her granddaughter's Christmas concert and how the granddaughter should have gotten the lead part.

When Ali finally reached the counter, she was greeted by a young clerk who looked barely out of high school. Her light brown hair appeared that it had not been brushed that morning as it fell into her eyes, and she wore just a hint of lip gloss. The girl looked tired, her shoulders slouched, as if the holiday season had already drained her enthusiasm for the job.

"Hi! Three books of candy cane stamps, please," Ali requested with a friendly smile, hoping a little cheer might lighten the girl's day.

The clerk barely looked up as she replied, "I've only got one book of candy canes left. Want some nutcracker stamps?" Her tone was flat, and it was clear she wasn't in the mood to search the shelves.

Ali's heart sank a little. It was silly, really, how much she cared about the stamps, but the small details mattered to her during the holidays. Each decision, no matter how small, contributed to the magic. "Could you double-check? Please?" Ali asked, adding a touch of pleading to her voice.

The clerk barely glanced at the shelves. "Nope, just the one."

"Do you have any Christmas tree ones?" Ali asked, hoping for a backup plan.

Without a word, the clerk handed over a book of candy cane stamps and two Christmas trees, her movements robotic. Ali remained gracious, making a mental note to hit the post office before Thanksgiving next year to avoid the holiday rush.

She left the post office, stamps in hand, her mind already moving on to the next errand—the liquor store. At least there she wouldn't have to worry about them running out of what she needed.

To her surprise, the liquor store was practically deserted, a rare gift during the holiday season. An older man, likely in his sixties, stood nearby in a well-worn fedora, slowly turning a bottle of bourbon in his hands, appearing to make an important decision. At the front of the store, a clerk, a burly man with a thick beard and plaid shirt, was busy assembling a towering display of eggnog, stacking with precision. Ali grabbed a shopping cart, the wobbly wheels breaking the stillness, and began her mission. The holidays required careful stocking, and she wasn't about to be caught unprepared.

First up: two cases of beer. One for the upcoming holiday party and another for those inevitable moments when guests overstayed their welcome.

Next, a case of rich red wine—ideal for both cozy evenings by the fire and last-minute gifts. She tossed in a bottle of Irish cream, because nothing said Christmas quite like a splash in her morning coffee.

Vodka followed, needed for impromptu cocktail nights. Then came the eggnog. Tommy insisted on it every year, and though she rarely touched it, she usually indulged in a glass or two for tradition's sake.

Finally, four bottles of champagne made their way into the cart. The holidays deserved a proper toast, after all.

She silently prayed she wouldn't bump into anyone she knew as she walked the aisles. Her shopping cart grew fuller with each stop, and Ali glanced at the contents, wondering if it screamed "holiday survival kit" more than festive fun. She had just turned the corner to the register when a stroke of bad luck intervened.

"Mrs. Marin! Nice to see you," Ali blurted, caught off guard as Noah's first-grade teacher walked through the door, looking effortlessly composed in her camel-colored peacoat. Ali's heart sank as she tried to shield the over-stuffed basket with her body, but there was no hiding the overflowing cart of booze.

Mrs. Marin smiled warmly, as her eyes flickered to the cart. "Looks like you're still celebrating Thanksgiving."

Ali forced a laugh, feeling her cheeks flush with embarrassment. "Just restocking for Christmas. You know how it is."

Mrs. Marin chuckled lightly, "Oh, I understand. It's a busy time of year. Hope you enjoy your weekend."

"You, too!" Ali called, her voice an octave higher than usual as Mrs. Marin continued down the aisle. Ali hurried through the checkout, hoping to avoid another familiar face.

By the time she pulled into the driveway, she was more than ready to leave the awkward liquor store encounter behind. She turned off the engine and glanced at the house, prepared to walk into chaos. Instead, Tommy was still tinkering in the garage, now with Noah by his side, proudly sporting a miniature tool belt that Ali had bought him last Christmas. The little boy beamed up at his dad, holding a small hammer like it was the most important tool in the world.

Maddie, no surprise, was nowhere to be seen, likely hiding out in her room, eyes glued to her cell phone. Pierce, true to form, had not moved from his spot in front of the television, flipping back and forth between football games.

"Maddie, did you start cleaning up like I asked?" Ali called up the stairs, already knowing the answer.

Maddie poked her head out of her bedroom door, her face a mix of innocence and defensiveness. "I didn't know you'd be back so soon!"

Upstairs, the artificial playroom tree stood bare waiting for decorations, it was smaller, more chaotic, and far more personal than the pristine, themed tree Ali displayed downstairs. This was the kids' tree, adorned with homemade ornaments, each holding a story, each year adding to its charm. While Ali took pride in the carefully curated beauty of her main tree, the playroom tree tugged at her heart in a different way. After the kids went to bed, she often found herself sitting beside it, basking in the soft glow of its mismatched lights. It offered a quiet comfort, a gentle reminder of Christmases past and the fleeting moments that made each one unforgettable.

In the living room, the sound of football echoed through the hall. Ali leaned into the doorway, questioning Pierce. "How much longer?"

"Fourth quarter," Pierce mumbled, eyes glued to the screen, barely acknowledging her presence.

"You've got twenty minutes or until the game ends, whichever comes first," Ali said. "Start with the living room and kitchen. Maddie's doing upstairs. I want it all done so we can decorate this weekend."

Tommy had already unloaded the haul from the car and set the boxes of alcohol on the counter, a grin on his face. "Feeling festive?" he teased, holding up a bottle of champagne in each hand.

Ali laughed with him, "I like to be prepared. Guess who I ran into at the liquor store?"

"Who?" he dramatically answered like a friend excited to hear new gossip.

"Noah's teacher. Mrs. Marin," Ali said with a cringe.

"She was there, too," Tommy shrugged. "No big deal."

Ali groaned. "It *is* a big deal. She saw me with a cart full of alcohol. I mean, it's not like I drink it all myself, but now she probably thinks I spend my evenings passed out on the couch while Noah fends for himself."

Tommy chuckled. "You're overthinking it. She was probably there for the same reason you were—to stock up for the holidays."

Ali leaned against the counter, arms crossed. "I know that *logically,* but it's hard not to picture her sitting in the teachers' lounge, sipping coffee and whispering, 'You'll never believe who I saw at the liquor store.'"

Tommy set the bottle down and gave her a playful nudge. "Trust me, she's not giving you a second thought.

Besides, she probably had a cart full of wine herself."

Ali shot him a look. "She had just walked in the door but didn't grab a shopping cart. She was probably getting one bottle of wine, like a responsible adult."

Tommy laughed. "And you had a whole cart? Okay, maybe she *is* telling that story."

"Not helping!" Ali said, though she couldn't help but crack a smile.

Ali sighed and changed the subject as Noah entered the room, "I need the empty boxes for the Thanksgiving decorations. And can you bring the Christmas stuff down from the attic?"

Tommy straightened up, puffing out his chest like he was about to embark on a great adventure. "Let's go, Noah," he said, and with his trusty sidekick in tow, they marched off to the attic, ready to face the Christmas preparations head-on.

In the dining room, Ali carefully rolled the candlesticks in linen, her fingers working methodically to preserve each item as she packed away Thanksgiving. The porcelain pumpkin engraved with "Crawford" was her favorite, a gift from her mother-in-law years ago, and she wrapped it with extra bubble wrap, ensuring its safe storage. Packing away fall décor meant one thing: Christmas was officially beginning, and everything needed to be just right.

Two hours passed. The dining room table, once overflowing with the remnants of Thanksgiving, now stood bare and ready for a new holiday transformation. The kitchen, too, had been stripped of its autumn leaves and pumpkin-scented candles, replaced with the cold, empty counters that awaited a fresh touch of Christmas cheer.

With the Thanksgiving boxes neatly stacked and ready for the attic, it was time to bring down Christmas. But when she checked the garage and attic, Tommy was nowhere to be found.

"Tommy?" she called, expecting to hear him rummaging through the garage or clambering up the attic ladder. Silence. He wasn't in the garage or the attic, and when she called for him, there was no response.

Maddie and Noah sat cross-legged on the living room floor, giggling as they played Guess Who, a rare occurrence since Maddie started middle school last year. The scene softened her frustration for a moment; she loved seeing her kids play together without screens or distractions.

Ali continued to search for Tommy and soon heard the unmistakable sound of football blaring from the back porch. She slid open the back door, already knowing what she'd find. There they were—Tommy and Pierce, sprawled out on the outdoor couch, fully immersed in the game. Chip bags, empty beer, and soda cans were on the table beside them. She felt her jaw clench.

"Tommy, the Thanksgiving boxes are ready for the attic," Ali said, trying to keep her voice calm.

Tommy didn't look up. "Okay," he replied, eyes still glued to the screen as if he had not heard her.

Ali took a breath. "Can you do it now?"

"The game distracted me. I'll get to it, I promise." He stood up, kissed her cheek, and offered, "Want a beer? Join us."

Pierce, who had been lounging on the couch scrolling through his phone, looked up. "Yeah, Mom. Christmas magic will handle the boxes, and maybe Santa's elves have a cleaning service."

Ali shot him a withering glare. "Not helpful, Pierce."

Tommy smirked at their son's comment but quickly stifled it when Ali's glare shifted to him. "You're not the one doing it all!" she snapped, the edge in her voice sharp now. "I need more help, if I am ever going to get it all done this year."

Tommy exhaled, standing up straighter, "Hard to help when you don't trust us to do anything."

"What was that?" Ali snapped, her frustration steaming and threatening to boil over at any moment.

"Just that you don't seem to trust anyone else to help you. We are here, we can help, but it's like you don't want us to."

Pierce couldn't resist chiming in again. "Dad's got a point."

Ali turned to Pierce, not finding him funny at this moment. "When was the last time you tried to help?"

Pierce grinned, lifting his phone to scroll again. "I thought about it last year. That counts, right?"

Tommy attempted to stifle laughter, resulting in a loud snort. Ali felt like she might combust if he didn't keep his mouth shut.

Pierce shrugged, unfazed. "Hey, I'm just here for the cookies and the presents."

"Ugh," Ali growled. "You all have no idea what it takes to pull off Christmas," she shot back, her frustration sharp now, no longer contained. "All the things I have to do to make Christmas magical for everyone."

"Whoa, whoa, whoa." She had finally gained Tommy's full attention. "No one asked you to do all this for us or be this stressed out all the time during the holidays."

"Oh, really, what am I supposed to do then, Tommy? There are not elves coming to our house to just make Christmas happen." Her eyes shot at Pierce as he choked on his laugh. Reading the room and wanting nothing to do with his parents' fight, he tucked his phone in the front pocket of his sweater and slowly moved towards the door.

"You act like it's so hard to pull off Christmas, but if you just took a step back, I think you would realize that you are focusing on all the wrong things –"

"Are you serious?" Ali asked, cutting him off... "That is such a Tommy attitude."

"What's that supposed to mean?"

"That means you never appreciate the work and planning I put into this family."

"Now, c'mon, that is not fair, Ali." She could see the hurt on his face from her unfair and honestly untrue words, but she was angry, tired, and frustrated.

"You're right, I'm sorry, but I just feel as if I'm alone in all this right now," she admitted.

Tommy preferred the angry Ali to the upset Ali. "Okay,

how about this?" Tommy smirked, folding his arms across his chest. "Why don't you let me handle Christmas this year?"

Ali blinked, caught off guard. "What?"

"You heard me," Tommy said, his smirk growing. "I'll take care of everything you do for Christmas."

"No, no, that's not what I meant." Ali waved off the ludicrous idea.

"Ali," Tommy gently placed a stable hand on either shoulder. "Look at me... the whole thing, let me do it this year."

"Really?" Ali didn't look convinced. "You really think you can handle Christmas alone?"

"Okay, how about you take over my responsibilities?" he offered.

Ali raised an eyebrow. "Seriously?"

"Deal, sweetheart?" Tommy asked, holding out his hand with a grin that forced her to smile briefly and made her stomach turn simultaneously.

"Fine," Ali agreed, reluctantly shaking his hand.

Behind them, Maddie and Noah had joined Pierce in the doorway. Noah's eyes wide with worry, turned to his siblings and whispered, "Christmas is ruined."

CHAPTER 2

Ali

As Ali lay in bed Friday night, staring at the ceiling in the dark, a wave of panic crept over her. She had just handed over control of Christmas to Tommy, and now she was second-guessing every bit of it. Rolling from her left side to her right, her thoughts churned relentlessly, each passing minute piling more anxiety onto her chest.

Sure, this could teach Tommy just how much effort went into making the holidays run smoothly. That had been the whole point, hadn't it? But what if it didn't? What if everything went completely off the rails, and her carefully built traditions unraveled?

Ali squeezed her eyes shut, trying to will herself into sleep, but her mind wouldn't let go. She wasn't losing sleep because of the endless to-do list this time. No, this was worse. Now she couldn't control what would happen, and the uncertainty gnawed at her.

It felt like a lose-lose situation. If Tommy succeeded, would he think all her years of effort had been overblown? And if he failed, she'd be left to clean up the mess.

Ali sighed, flipping her pillow to the cool side. It was going to be a long night.

Tiptoeing down the stairs on Saturday morning, Ali expected the familiar sound of Noah's cartoons blasting in the living room. But as she reached the bottom step, she was greeted by an unexpected stillness. The only sound was the morning news, its dull commentary so different from the usual animated voices that filled the space.

A wave of curiosity washed over her. Odd, she thought, as the smell of freshly brewed coffee hit her senses. She rounded the corner and entered the kitchen where Tommy sat at the kitchen table, casually playing the New York Times games on his phone, completely relaxed, solving the daily Wordle with a fresh cup of coffee beside him, and his hair still tousled from sleep. The soft, early light filtered through the window, casting a golden glow over the room, making everything feel oddly serene. No kids were in sight, no cereal scattered across the counter, no cartoons on the television. It was as if she had stepped into a completely different household, one that was calm and quiet, very different from their usual Saturday.

Ali stood in the doorway for a moment, taking in the scene, her brow furrowing in confusion. It wasn't that Tommy never got up early, he often did, but this felt... different.

"Good morning," she finally said, her voice tentative as she crossed the room.

Tommy looked up from his phone, flashing her a quick smile with his warm, boyish grin and twinkling blue eyes. "Morning," he said, taking a sip of his coffee.

Ali moved around the kitchen, "Noah?" she asked, grabbing a glass from the cabinet.

"He's still asleep," Tommy replied, glancing up briefly. "First time he's slept this late in months."

Ali opened the refrigerator and poured herself a glass of orange juice, ignoring the freshly brewed coffee on the counter. She took a sip, the tartness cutting through her simmering irritation. It wasn't lost on her that she consciously avoided the coffee Tommy had made. It was petty, sure, but she was angry and didn't care.

Tommy sat there serenely, scrolling through his phone with the ease of someone who had all the time in the world. His posture was relaxed as if it were any other day. Tommy always had a hint of stubble on his strong jawline, giving him a slightly rugged look, and his wavy brown hair tended to fall just a little out of place, something Ali constantly wanted to fix, but wouldn't dare change. Today, however, it bothered her a little more than normal.

How did he manage to stay so collected? Ali envied that about him. Tommy had this uncanny ability to shut off the noise, ignore the mental lists, and just exist in the moment. Meanwhile, her mind was a constant hum of activity, ticking through the endless tasks that always seemed to pile up.

While Ali was perfectly polished, Tommy's style leaned more casual and relaxed—well-worn jeans, fitted t-shirts, and flannel shirts with the sleeves rolled up. He could clean up well when the occasion called for it, but he was happiest when he was comfortable and himself. The perfect Yang to Ali's Ying, Tommy had a way of softening her edges, bringing out her playful, spontaneous side. And though he didn't show it in the same way Ali did, he was fiercely devoted to his family, his easygoing exterior hiding a heart of pure gold.

As she leaned against the counter, her eyes fell on the edge of a crumpled piece of paper, the unfinished to-do list from yesterday. It sat there mocking her with its unchecked boxes and half-scribbled reminders. She picked it up, smoothing the wrinkles with her fingers, and slid it across the counter toward Tommy.

"Maybe this will light a fire under you," she said, trying to keep her tone casual but unable to hide the edge of frustration in her voice. Tommy glanced at the list but then continued his games. Grabbing the pancake mix, she moved back to the counter and began preparing the batter. The silence between them felt heavier than she intended, so she spoke up, trying to sound as casual as possible.

"So...what's the plan for today?" Ali asked, her tone deliberately nonchalant as she stirred the batter. In truth, she was trying to gauge what Tommy was thinking.

Tommy looked up from his phone with a grin. "While *you're* getting the Christmas decorations down from the attic, I'll watch more football."

Ali's mind flashed back to last night's argument. It had all started because he *hadn't* gotten the decorations down. She bit her lip, focusing on stirring the pancake mix, the tension in her shoulders creeping higher.

Twenty minutes later, the smell of bacon drew the kids from their rooms like bees to honey. Maddie, Pierce, and Noah shuffled into the silent kitchen, grabbed juice, and settled around the table. The scene was so familiar, so comforting, that Ali's irritation eased just a bit. Breakfast was their sacred family time, with Pierce drenching his plate until everything was a soggy mess and Noah dunking his pancakes in syrup. Maddie, always different, ate hers dry.

Halfway through breakfast, Noah looked up from his plate and asked, "Are we getting the Christmas tree today?"

Ali started to answer, "No, not today," but before she could finish, Tommy jumped in.

"Yes, we're getting one today," he said, his voice firm but playful.

Ali frowned, caught off guard. "We always get the tree on Sunday. We're not ready yet."

Tommy raised an eyebrow, a smirk tugging at the corner of his mouth. "I'm in charge of Christmas now, remember?" he teased. "But you're right about one thing, you've got plenty of decorations to dig out. Today is football day. Tomorrow is tree day."

Ali glared at her husband, pushed her half-eaten pancake into the garbage, and left the room, retreating upstairs to take a quick shower. By the time she came back down, dressed in a festive shirt that read *On the Nice List*, she had calmed herself.

As Ali stepped into the kitchen, she did a double take. The kids were... cleaning? That never happened without a little incentive. "Earning some Mom bucks?" she asked, raising a skeptical eyebrow, waiting for the catch.

"Nope," Noah said proudly, smiling at his mother with his toothless grin. "Dad told us to help you."

Ali rolled her eyes, muttering under her breath, "I don't need help... He's the one who's going to need it." Her words were sharp, but the smile tugging at her lips betrayed her. She watched as Pierce wiped down the counters and Maddie half-heartedly stored the extra pancakes in a freezer bag. She had to admit, seeing the kids pitch in was nice.

Determined to follow through on her one task for the day, Ali made a list, more for her sanity than anything else.

Saturday:

☐ *Bring Christmas decorations down from the attic.*

Simple. Straightforward. Nothing to panic about.

She marched upstairs to the attic door, barely reaching the cord to release the ladder. Except the ladder didn't come down. Frowning, she tried again, her fingertips pinching the end of the cord. Nothing. A few more tries later, she practically jumped to get a better grip.

Suddenly, Noah appeared in the doorway, wide-eyed and curious. "Mommy, do you want to use the stool from the bathroom? That's how I reach the sink."

Ali sighed, her hands on her hips, then smiled. "That's a great idea, Buddy."

A few minutes later, thanks to Noah's quick thinking and a bathroom stool, Ali finally managed to pull the attic stairs down. She climbed into the dusty space, the air was stale and heavy with the scent of forgotten cardboard and insulation. She immediately realized her mistake, she'd forgotten to grab a flashlight. Grumbling, she felt along the wall, her fingers grazed cobwebs that made her yelp and jerk her hand back. She hated spiders. *Hated* them.

When her fingers finally found the light switch, she flipped it on, and a dim, flickering bulb cast just enough light to reveal the attic's contents. Rows of neatly labeled boxes greeted her, a haphazard archive of family life.

The boxes were coated in a fine layer of dust, making Ali sneeze, their sharpie-scrawled labels barely visible. Her irritation mounted as she skimmed over Tommy's so-called organizational system. *Halloween: Costumes & Pumpkins* was wedged between *Easter: Baskets & Eggs* and an unlabeled box she could only assume was random junk Tommy didn't know what to do with.

After a good ten minutes of searching, Ali found the red bins marked "Christmas." How did he think putting Christmas decorations next to the 4th of July bin made any sense?

Grinning triumphantly, Ali grabbed the handle of one of the bins and gave it a hearty tug toward the attic stairs. As soon as she pulled, the grin vanished. The bin barely budged, its weight catching her completely off guard.

She frowned and gave it another yank, her hands straining against the cold plastic. It was heavier than she'd remembered—packed to the brim with Christmas garland, wreaths, and lights. How did Tommy get these bins up and down the stairs so easily? She climbed down the ladder to assess the situation, glaring up at the stack of bins. Eight of them. There was no way she could do it by herself.

Then, inspiration struck. Pierce. Heading downstairs, she found him staring into the fridge, probably looking for his second breakfast.

"Hey, Pierce, feel like using those muscles to help your mom?" Ali asked, trying to sound casual as she wiped a stray strand of hair from her face. She knew the teenage look he gave her all too well, the skeptical raise of the brow as he barely glanced up.

Ali smirked as she went in for the win. "How about pizza for lunch?"

That did it. "Fine," he said as he smirked at his mother and closed the refrigerator "But only cuz I'm starving."

With the bribe accepted, they tackled the bins together, one at a time. The operation quickly turned into a comedy routine as they tried to maneuver the massive boxes down the attic ladder. Ali went first, carefully guiding the first bin step by step, but halfway down, it tilted dangerously in her hands.

"Uh, Mom, you good?" Pierce called, as he watched her wobble.

"Totally fine," she said through gritted teeth, though her sweaty grip told a different story.

Before the bin could crash, Pierce lunged forward and grabbed the edge, steadying it just as Ali nearly lost her balance.

"Guess my workout program's working," he quipped, flashing a grin as he set the box down.

They continued, both panting by the time the last bin landed in the family room. Ali collapsed onto the couch, feeling like her muscles had turned to jelly. Meanwhile, Pierce stood tall, making a big show of flexing his biceps.

"Easy," he said, his voice dripping with exaggeration. "I could've done that in my sleep."

Ali rolled her eyes but laughed. "You're a lifesaver, Hulk. Ready for pizza?"

Pierce gave her a half-smile, clearly satisfied with his reward. As he made his way toward the stairs, he called out to his mom, "Pepperoni *and* sausage. Don't forget the sausage, or this was all for nothing."

Ali shook her head, grinning as she wiped her forehead with her sleeve. Tommy might think football was the highlight of the day, but she'd just scored her own small victory.

As she leaned back into the couch, she made a mental note: Epsom salt bath tonight. She'd *earned* it.

CHAPTER 3

Tommy

Tommy spent most of Friday and Saturday glued to football games on television, fully embracing the freedom of his four-day weekend. With a beer in hand and his feet propped up, he looked like a man without a care in the world. No honey-do lists to tackle, no hauling heavy boxes of decorations, and no frantic trips to the hardware store. Ali had given him the reins for the holiday.

When he finally wandered into the kitchen on Saturday evening, the comforting smells of chicken soup with homemade noodles greeted him. Ali stood at the stove, flipping grilled cheese sandwiches to pair with the soup.

"Hey, honey, it smells amazing in here," Tommy said, admiring his wife. Ali's honey-blonde hair was always styled to perfection; wearing it in soft waves gave her a polished look even in the comfort of her own home. There was an inviting energy about her, from the way she tilted her head when she listened intently to someone's story to the way her laughter filled a room with genuine warmth. Ali was the kind of person people naturally gravitate toward, a woman who seemed to have everything perfectly in order, but who was grounded and approachable.

Ali turned around to face him, a smile on her face, but her typical warm expression replaced an annoyed look in her hazel eyes. "Since I don't have Christmas prep to worry about, I decided to use my time cooking dinner." There it was, the subtle dig. Ali was reminding him, without directly saying it, that she would usually be neck-deep in Christmas tasks by now. "The Christmas decorations are in the family room when you're ready for them," Ali added while flipping a grilled cheese sandwich to keep it from sticking to the pan.

Tommy glanced toward the family room doorway, not in any rush to get started. "Thanks. I'll get to it after dinner," he replied.

Walking into the family room, he was immediately taken aback by the stack of red bins piled nearly to the ceiling. *Have we always had this many?* He wondered how Ali had managed to get them downstairs. He paused for a minute remembering how much trouble he had getting them back into the attic last January. Curious, he peeked into the top bin, which contained something that looked like either a tablecloth or a tree skirt. He closed it quickly, this could definitely wait until after dinner.

Dinner was as good as it smelled, and even Noah cleared his plate, which was impressive given his current chicken nugget-only phase. Once Tommy and Ali finished the dishes together, the rest of the family settled into the playroom to watch *The Grinch* and Tommy returned to the family room. He felt a twinge of longing to join as he watched his family get cozy, but for him, it was time to tackle the bins.

The first bin he opened revealed their treasured nativity set, carefully wrapped in layers of bubble wrap. Tommy slowed, gently unwrapping each piece. He smiled when he held the hand-painted ceramic figures, each one a little reminder of Ali's tradition to let the kids help set it up. Every year, they chose different spots for the figurines, Maddie always insisted the donkey stand directly next to baby Jesus, while Noah liked to make the wise men line up in a neat, military-style row.

Tommy placed the pieces on a floating shelf in the family room, making sure they were centered, demoting the antique clock that usually sat there to storage. The nativity deserved the prime spot; however, he made a mental note to let the kids rearrange the pieces in the morning.

Next came the bin filled with the family ornaments, which ironically coincided with a beautiful acoustic version of "Somewhere in My Memory" starting to play softly from the kitchen. Tommy couldn't help but sit down and sift through them, getting lost in the memories. There was the ornament from their trip to Disney World two years ago, complete with Mickey Mouse ears, packed tightly next to the little ceramic heart with "Our First Christmas" written on it from the year he and Ali got married. He smiled as he found the ornaments the kids had made, handprints turned into Santa faces, popsicle stick reindeer, and glitter-covered stars.

One ornament in particular made Tommy stop in his tracks, a small photo frame with a picture of Pierce as a toddler, dressed in his Christmas pajamas. He had a childish grin that stretched from ear to ear, and it reminded Tommy just how quickly time was flying. Pierce was a junior in high school but with that ornament in Tommy's hand, Pierce still felt like his little boy.

After a trip down memory lane, Tommy moved on to the next bin. This one was filled with knickknacks, random holiday decorations that Ali usually spread throughout the house. He found the reindeer cookie jar and immediately filled it with the Oreos that were hidden in the pantry. It wasn't homemade like Ali would have baked, but it was something.

He also came across the Santa and Mrs. Claus salt and pepper shakers, gifts from Ali's sister, that always managed to make their way onto the kitchen island. He placed them down, admiring their cheerful expressions, then set up the green tablecloth with gold candlesticks in the center of the kitchen table. He was determined to make the house feel festive.

In the next bin, Tommy found the dancing Batman doll who wore a Santa hat and played Jingle Bells, Batman Smells. Last year, Noah had discovered it and hysterically laughed so hard he had fallen over. The sight of his youngest son's joy made Tommy chuckle even now, so he placed the Christmas Batman in the living room where Noah would see it first thing in the morning.

Then came the framed photos of Christmases past, pictures of the kids meeting Santa, their annual family portraits in front of the tree, and snapshots of Christmas mornings over the years. Tommy lined them up along the mantel, replacing the everyday pictures with these seasonal memories.

Garland and twinkling lights were next, strung along the built-in shelves. Tommy was proud of how it turned out, even managing to weave the lights in and out of the books without knocking anything over. And although the Christmas train had not worked in years, Tommy gave it a place of honor across the center shelf, proudly displayed in front of the now-replaced family photos.

Ali and the kids had gone to bed hours ago, but Tommy was still at it, determined to get everything just right. Exhaustion was starting to creep in, but the house was beginning to feel like Christmas. It wasn't Ali's perfectly curated holiday masterpiece, but it was... *his*.

He had even draped a red and green plaid blanket, one he didn't remember ever seeing, across the back of the couch. It added a cozy touch, making the room feel even warmer. The last task of the night was hanging the stockings. He took care to line them up evenly across the mantel, Ali's elf figurines perched happily above them.

Around 2 a.m., Tommy finally called it a night. The house was transformed, decked out in holiday cheer. He restacked the empty bins, stashed them in the garage, and left the ornament boxes for tomorrow. Tommy looked around, exhausted but satisfied.

CHAPTER 4

Ali

Ali was the second person to rise on Sunday morning, with Noah earning back his first-place title after sleeping a little late the prior morning. Noah was curled up on the couch, rewatching *The Grinch* and munching on cereal straight from the box, the typical Sunday morning scene. What wasn't typical was the Christmas explosion that had happened overnight. When Noah saw his mom, he squealed with delight, "It's Christmas, Mommy!"

Ali could barely get out any words, "it sure is," she mumbled. She stood there, trying to process the chaos around her. Snowflake decorations were mixed with Santas, gingerbread men combined with elves—those silly elves she only put out when her mother, who gifted them to her, visited were now occupying her beautiful mantle, which was usually reserved for fresh flowers and candles.

It looked like the Christmas bins had exploded all over the house with no rhyme or reason.

Ali smiled, unable to resist Noah's enthusiasm. "Daddy decorated," she said, deciding that Tommy deserved the praise from the kids.

"Did I hear my name?" Tommy asked, walking into the kitchen.

"Daddy, look at all the Christmas!" Noah yelled joyfully.

"I know, buddy. I'm glad you like it," Tommy said with a big smile.

Ali noticed how genuine that smile was, Tommy had enjoyed decorating. The memory of the night before came rushing back, and Ali found herself smiling, too. While Tommy had been busy transforming their home into a holiday wonderland, Ali had unexpectedly slowed down for the first time in weeks. She'd spent the evening curled up with the kids, watching *The Grinch* and sharing popcorn. For once, she hadn't been checking lists or planning her next move; she'd simply enjoyed the moment. It was a feeling she wasn't used to, but one she wouldn't soon forget.

As she made her way into the kitchen, she was taken aback to see the dining room tablecloth spread out on the kitchen table. The golden candlesticks, a cherished wedding gift, were also placed there. Typically, she would meticulously arrange these items on the dining room table, not on the everyday kitchen table.

In her mind, when she handed over the Christmas

duties to Tommy, she had never imagined that the decorations would be in the wrong places. She had assumed he would just follow the layout she had carefully perfected over the years.

Ali was unable to focus on breakfast or planning her day; she hurriedly made herself a cup of coffee using the Keurig. She needed the caffeine quicker than the time it would take to brew a whole pot. As the aroma of fresh coffee filled the kitchen, she took a moment to savor the first sip, hoping it would help her gather her thoughts. Standing by the kitchen counter, she pondered whether Tommy would notice if she subtly rearranged a few items in the room, contemplating each movement with a sense of cautious deliberation.

About an hour later, Pierce and Maddie joined them for a breakfast of sausage, eggs, and biscuits. As they ate, the kids chatted about the decorations scattered around the house.

"Who put the *Baking Christmas Cheer* gingerbread kitchen towel in the bathroom?" Maddie asked, giggling.

"Obviously, someone who doesn't understand the difference between a bathroom and a kitchen," Pierce said, smirking.

Maddie snorted. "It's probably the same person who thought winning an 'Ugly Christmas Sweater' award was a life achievement worth displaying in the living room."

Noah, joining his siblings in their banter, pretended to stroke his chin. "Hmm, I wonder who that could be…"

Tommy raised an eyebrow, clearly amused. "Careful,

or I'll dig out the pictures of you guys in matching reindeer pajamas with glowing noses from 2019 and *those* will go on the shelf next to my award."

Pierce grinned. "You wouldn't?"

Tommy's eyes twinkled. "Try me."

The table erupted in laughter, and even Ali couldn't help but join in, grateful for the lighthearted start to the day.

Changing the subject, Tommy announced, "After breakfast, get dressed. We're heading to the Christmas tree farm."

Noah let out an excited cheer, and even Maddie and Pierce gave Tommy a smile.

"I'll clean up the kitchen so you can get ready," Tommy offered to Ali, stacking plates as he spoke.

Ali nodded and headed upstairs, pausing for a moment to glance around at the decorations again. Maybe they'll grow on me, she thought, a small smile tugging at her lips.

By noon, the family was packed into the Suburban and on their way to Southern Hollow Christmas Tree Farm, a scenic 30-minute drive from their home in Fairhope, Alabama. Though there were closer places to buy a tree, it was a tradition for the Crawfords to make the trip to Southern Hollow, and this year was no different.

When they arrived, hard-working teenagers dressed as elves greeted them with steaming cups of hot chocolate, while "Holly Jolly Christmas" played softly from speakers hidden around the farm. After quickly finishing her drink,

Maddie bolted toward the trees, determined to choose the family's tree, with Noah, sporting a hot chocolate mustache and an untied shoe, racing after her.

"Here we go," Ali sighed as she jogged to catch up.

Maddie, of course, picked out a tree that belonged in the center of town, not a suburban living room. "Absolutely not, that one wouldn't fit through our front door," Ali explained.

Pierce pointed out a small, scraggly tree missing most of its branches. "It's a Charlie Brown tree!" he laughed.

"No way, how are we going to hang decorations on that?" Ali countered.

Then Noah, with his usual enthusiasm, chose a fat tree, shorter than the others but fuller. Ali wrinkled her nose, about to say no again, when Maddie piped up, "You're no fun, Mom."

Was she suggesting that Ali was boring, unlike Tommy with his unrestricted decorating? *I can be fun too,* she thought.

"Okay, let's go with Noah's pick this year," she said, resigning herself to the best of the three options. *Tommy has to figure out how to decorate that wide tree*, she laughed to herself.

She flagged down an attendant and asked for help getting the tree loaded onto the Suburban. Tommy, usually in charge of the tree logistics, stood back this time, smirking in the distance.

The attendant, probably a college student home for the holidays, asked, "Mrs. Crawford, do you have ropes to tie down the tree?"

Ali froze. "Ropes?"

"Yes, ma'am, to secure the tree," he replied, now less cheerful.

Ali realized she hadn't thought of that. She had brought snacks, water, tip money, and even Noah's iPad for the car ride, but no rope. She glanced at Tommy, who was keeping his distance, standing near the restrooms, grinning smugly.

Of course, he hadn't mentioned needing rope. Probably on purpose, she thought, shaking her head.

"I don't have any," she admitted. "Do you sell some here?"

"We sell bungee rope for $40 at the hot chocolate stand," the attendant said, his tone now bordering on annoyed. "Or you could head up to Ace Hardware—it's just one exit away."

Leaving without a tree was not an option. "I'll be right back," she sighed and headed to the hot chocolate stand.

Thirty minutes and an extra $40 later, the tree was strapped securely to the top of the Suburban, its branches swaying lightly in the breeze as they climbed into their seats. Tommy glanced at the crumpled receipt in Ali's hand with a mischievous expression.

"So," he started, leaning back in his seat and crossing his arms, "how much was that bungee rope and twine?" His tone was teasing, but Ali could already tell where this was headed.

"It doesn't matter," she replied, trying to keep her voice

casual as she stuffed the receipt deeper into her pocket. She started to change the station on the radio, hoping to distract him.

"Oh, it definitely matters," Tommy chuckled, glancing sideways at her, clearly enjoying himself. "Come on, how much?"

Ali glared at him, knowing full well he wouldn't let it go. "I'm not going to say," she replied, her jaw tightening. "We have a tree—that's what matters."

Tommy's grin widened, and he shook his head with exaggerated disbelief. "You probably paid double what it costs at a hardware store, didn't you?" He leaned forward, peering over at her as if he could read the price in her eyes.

"Tommy, stop," Ali exhaled, "Do you want the tree or not?"

Ali's mind was turning over as they drove home, *how am I going to get that thing inside and on the stand?* she wondered, glancing at the massive tree strapped to the roof. She knew she would need Pierce's help again, and that meant she'd owe him something big—probably more than just pizza this time.

*When t*hey pulled into the driveway, Ali asked Noah and Maddie to head inside and clear away any toys in the family room to make space for the tree. "Pierce, can you stay with me for a minute?

Tommy chuckled from the driver's seat, "I'll go inside and get a seat for the show "

Ali shot him a glare but didn't dignify the joke with

a response.

Turning to Pierce, she said, "I need you to go next door and ask Jake and Ryan to help us get the tree inside. I'll pay them both twenty dollars."

The Wilkins' twin boys, Jake and Ryan, lived next door. They were 14, a couple of years younger than Pierce, the trio had been inseparable when they were younger but when Pierce started high school, the boys had stopped hanging out as much. Ali continued to hope their friendship would reignite as the twins got older. Between the four of them, she knew they could get the tree inside.

Pierce's eyes lit up. "What about me?"

"I'll pay you twenty also." Ali did a quick mental tally of the extra costs this Christmas swap was racking up.

A few minutes later, Pierce returned with Jake and Ryan in tow and ready to help. They wasted no time getting to work, but moving the tree was more challenging than expected. As they untied the bungee cords, the tree rolled off the Suburban, straight toward Pierce, who wasn't prepared to catch the 60-pound tree. Both Pierce and the tree went tumbling to the ground.

"Pierce!" Ali called out as she and the boys scrambled to lift the tree off him. It wasn't easy; the weight and awkward shape made it a struggle, but eventually, they managed to roll it off his chest.

Pierce groaned as he sat up, brushing off needles from his jacket. "This is worth more than twenty dollars, Mom," he grumbled, giving her a half-hearted glare. Ali chuckled;

thankful he wasn't hurt.

With Pierce back on his feet, they all regrouped, determined to get the tree inside. It took careful planning and a lot of grunting, but with a bit of teamwork, Ryan and Jake held the bottom, Pierce took the middle, and Ali guided from the top; they managed to carry the tree through the front door, needles dropping along the way.

Ali wiped her brow, her arms already sore, but she couldn't help but feel proud.

CHAPTER 5

Tommy

Tommy's eyebrows shot up as he watched Jake and Ryan, the neighborhood twins, hauling the Christmas tree into the living room with Pierce. He hadn't even considered that Ali might call in reinforcements from outside the family. Clever, he thought.

Leaning casually against the doorframe, Tommy folded his arms and watched the organized chaos unfold. The tree tipped precariously for a moment, prompting Ali to bark out precise instructions on how to stabilize it.

When the boys finally settled the tree into the stand, Tommy sauntered over to Ali, "So," he began, his tone light but curious, "how'd you convince the boys to pitch in so willingly?"

Ali paused just long enough to make Tommy's grin widen.

"They're just sweet boys," she replied smoothly,

brushing off imaginary pine needles from her sweater. "They know how much Christmas means to me. They wanted to help."

"Uh-huh," Tommy said, his eyebrows arching higher. "Sweet boys, huh? All three of them, just jumping at the chance to haul a tree inside on a Sunday afternoon?"

Ali straightened up and gave him a pointed look. "I don't need to reveal all my tricks, the tree is inside. What's your point?"

Tommy chuckled, not bothering to hide his skepticism. "No point, just impressed. You're full of surprises, you know that?"

"Quick thinking," Ali said with a tight smile. "You should be thanking me."

"Oh, I will," Tommy said, amused. "I can't wait to tell Skip about the little deal we made. You know, switching Christmas duties and all. The cat's officially out of the bag now."

Ali's face froze for a fraction of a second, but she recovered quickly, waving him off. She had not considered what her friends and neighbors would think of this crazy arrangement. "I'm sure he'll find it hilarious. Now, you have a tree to decorate," she reminded Tommy.

Tommy shook his head, still grinning as he turned back to the living room. Ali might be a mastermind, but he was pretty sure she wasn't telling him the full story.

Early Monday morning, Tommy strolled into the radio station where he had worked for the last eight years, still rubbing his eyes after the chaotic long weekend. As he swiped his ID badge at the entrance, the familiar buzz of the studio greeted him. The rhythmic hum of computers, the faint sound of the current broadcast playing in the background, and the rich aroma of fresh coffee brewing in the kitchenette all made him feel at home.

His buddy Luis, the morning disc jockey, was already on air. The soundproof glass of the booth revealed Luis in his usual energetic form, gesturing wildly as he cracked jokes with a caller. Luis, with his signature wide-brimmed trucker hat and animated personality, was a station favorite. They had worked together for years, and though Luis got most of the attention on air, Tommy's quiet, steady hand as producer was the backbone of the station.

"Tommy!" Luis called out through the speaker as soon as the mic was off. "How was your Thanksgiving man?"

"I barely survived it," Tommy replied with a chuckle, setting down his bag and grabbing a fresh cup of hot coffee. "Made a deal with Ali, I'd take over her Christmas planning, and she'd handle all the other things I usually do. Big mistake."

Luis laughed. "Whoa, I bet she's not happy."

"She's... tolerating it," Tommy said with a smirk. "I'm just trying to get through the next few weeks without ruining anything too badly."

As they chatted, Tommy's phone vibrated on the desk. He glanced at the screen and saw the name: *Mrs. Marin*, Noah's teacher. His stomach dropped. Ali had something on her list about Noah's class holiday party; she must have given his number to Mrs. Marin as part of this new "you're-in-charge-of-Christmas" deal. He picked up the call, bracing himself.

"Hello, Mr. Crawford?" came the upbeat voice on the other end.

"Yes, speaking. Mrs. Marin, right?" Tommy responded, keeping his tone polite.

"That's right. I just wanted to touch base about Noah's classroom holiday party next Friday. Mrs. Crawford mentioned you'd be handling the planning."

Tommy blinked. Of course, she did.

"Sure, yeah. What can I do?" He grabbed a pen and notepad, trying to sound like he knew what was coming.

"Well," Mrs. Marin began, her voice growing even more cheerful, "we have some special requests this year! There are three Jewish students in the class, so we're incorporating Hanukkah into the celebration. We'll need some Hanukkah decorations—maybe a menorah, dreidels."

Tommy nodded, scribbling "Hanukkah décor" on the notepad.

"Oh, and for the craft project, I was thinking we could do an elaborate holiday scene diorama. Each child can make a piece of it, and we'll glue it all together at the party!"

"Diorama?" Tommy repeated, writing it down, though the idea made his head spin. "Got it."

"And one more thing," Mrs. Marin continued. "We'll need to provide a gluten-free dessert option. One of the students has celiac, and we want to make sure everyone can enjoy the treats."

Gluten-free dessert. Tommy wasn't even sure what gluten really was, but he wrote it down anyway.

"Sounds... great," Tommy said, trying to sound enthusiastic. "I'll, uh, get on that."

"Wonderful! Thanks so much for helping out, Mr. Crawford. Noah's lucky to have such an involved dad." Mrs. Marin hung up, leaving Tommy staring at his hastily scribbled notes.

Luis, who had been watching the whole exchange, grinned from the sound booth. He flipped off his mic and strolled over to Tommy, "Classroom party, huh? Sounds like you're screwed, my friend. Hope you know what you're doing."

"I'm trapped," Tommy muttered. "Ali handed this whole thing off to me. Now I've got to plan for Christmas and Hanukkah, figure out some complicated arts and crafts project, and find a gluten-free dessert. What even *is* gluten, Luis?"

Luis laughed. "Man, you're in deep. But hey, at least you've got a radio station at your disposal. You could do a whole segment on this— 'Holiday Planning for Dads Who Have No Clue.'"

Tommy groaned. "I just need to survive this party. Ali's going to love hearing about this later."

Luis patted him on the back. "You've got this, man. And if you need help finding gluten-free cookies, my cousin is a baker. She'll hook you up."

Tommy smiled, feeling slightly better. "I might just take you up on that."

As he settled into his routine at the station, reviewing schedules and fielding calls, Tommy's mind kept drifting back to the looming party: a menorah, a diorama, and gluten-free desserts.

As Tommy reached for his coffee, trying to focus on tomorrow's show, he was about to dive into the day's work when his phone buzzed with a text.

Did you hear from Mrs. Marin yet? It came along with a wink emoji.

It was Ali, cheekily referencing the ambush Tommy had just survived. He smirked, shaking his head as he typed back.

Yep, I'm officially on classroom party duty. Thanks for the heads up.

You're welcome, she replied quickly, and Tommy could almost see the mischievous grin on her face through the screen. He wasn't about to admit that the call had left him rattled. But before he could put his phone down, another message came through.

When are we taking the kids to see Santa?

Tommy paused. He had completely forgotten about that part of the holiday routine. There was always a special evening dedicated to visiting Santa, complete with festive outfits, and a very specific photo Ali loved to capture every year. Noah would be the most excited, while Maddie and Pierce would play along for the youngest Crawford, who still believed in the Santa magic.

I'll check the schedule today, he typed back.

Ali's short reply came almost instantly. *Perfect!*

Tommy sighed and tried to focus on work, but Ali wasn't done yet.

Did you reach out to the church to pick an angel from the angel tree? came the next message.

His stomach tightened a little. That was another thing he hadn't gotten to yet. Every year, they'd pick a child in need from the angel tree at their church and buy gifts for them. It was one of the family's favorite traditions, and missing it was out of the question.

I'll call today, he typed back quickly.

You're the best, Ali replied.

Tommy shook his head, chuckling softly. She had a way of making it sound easy, even when he felt like he was drowning in holiday obligations. He glanced at the calendar on his desk, realizing just how packed the next few weeks were going to be. Between work, decorating the Christmas tree, the classroom party, and now finding an angel to sponsor, it was going to take a miracle to get through it all.

As he returned to his tasks, Tommy couldn't help but think about how effortless Ali made everything seem when she was running Christmas. Now that it was on him, he was starting to appreciate just how much she handled every year.

CHAPTER 6

Ali

Ali sat in her office at the community college, staring at her computer screen but barely processing the words in front of her. The usual rhythm of advising students about resumes and career paths had been interrupted by her constant thoughts about Christmas. She sat at her desk, tapping her pen against the edge of her keyboard, picturing the tangle of Santas and gingerbread men currently taking over her living room. Tommy's decorating "skills" had turned her usually serene holiday display into something resembling a Christmas flea market gone wrong.

A gentle tap on the door broke her already broken concentration. Rachel, her colleague and longtime friend, peeked inside, her curly hair bouncing gently as she smiled. "Hey, are we still on for the Christmas Farmer's

Market on Saturday?"

Ali frowned and shook her head. "I'm skipping my usual flower and produce run this year. Tommy's taking charge of everything holiday-related—decorating, cooking, even the gifts."

Rachel's expression froze. She blinked a few times, seemingly trying to process this unbelievable piece of information. "I'm sorry, Tommy? Your Tommy?"

Ali nodded, sensing the disbelief herself. "Yeah, it's part of this... switch we made. He's managing Christmas this year, and I'm letting it happen."

Rachel's mouth dropped open. "This... this doesn't sound real. You? Giving up control? I mean, come on, Ali, the woman who has color-coded lists for her color-coded lists? The one who alphabetizes her spices for fun? You're telling me you're letting Tommy run Christmas?"

Rachel smirked, shaking her head. "I don't know, Ali. You've managed Christmas like a well-oiled machine for years. Can you seriously just sit back and let Tommy run the show?"

Ali laughed. "Look, it hasn't been easy. He's already swapped out my elegant holiday wreath for this light-up monstrosity with plastic snowflakes. But I'm hanging in there."

Rachel let out a soft laugh, clearly amused. "You're a better woman than me. I'd lose my mind after a day of not calling the shots."

Ali shrugged, a playful smile on her face. "We'll see if

I can last until Christmas."

Rachel leaned back in her chair; arms crossed. "You should still come to the farmer's market with me on Saturday. Even if you're not buying anything, you can help me shop." She shot Ali a knowing grin, fully aware that her friend wouldn't be able to resist doing some shopping of her own.

Ali shook her head. "Okay, okay, I'll go but I'm not buying anything this year. I told Tommy I wouldn't meddle, and I meant it."

Rachel tilted her head, studying her like she was some rare, exotic animal. "I don't know if I should be impressed or concerned."

Ali shrugged. "A little of both, probably."

Rachel raised an eyebrow, clearly skeptical. "You expect me to believe you'll walk through a holiday market and not buy a single thing? No flowers? No fancy cheeses? Not even a cinnamon-scented candle?"

"Not a single thing," Ali said, holding up a finger for emphasis. "I'm there purely for moral support. Plus, I need to bring Pierce, it has been our tradition since he was five. I only have a few more Christmas markets left with him before he's off to college."

Rachel smirked. "Just wait until you see those poinsettias. I give it five minutes before you're sneaking a pot into your trunk and swearing Tommy will never notice."

Ali laughed. "I'm serious! I've made a deal, and I'm sticking to it."

"Uh-huh. We'll see how long that lasts," Rachel said with a playful grin. "Saturday at 10?"

"We'll be there," Ali said, throwing her hands up in mock defeat. "But I'm not buying anything. You'll see."

As Rachel stood up, she gave Ali one last look. "I don't know how you're doing it, Ali. If my husband were in charge of Christmas, I'd be in the garage hyperventilating into a paper bag by now."

Ali chuckled. "Trust me, the paper bag is not out of the question yet." Letting go was proving harder than she'd ever imagined, but she was determined to see this through. She could survive one Tommy-led Christmas. Probably.

After Rachel left, Ali turned back to her computer, but her focus had evaporated completely. She grabbed her phone, scrolled through Pinterest, her feed filled with beautiful Christmas tablescapes, handmade wreaths, and perfectly frosted sugar cookies. A pang of longing hit her hard. Normally, she'd be knee-deep in DIY projects by now—hand-painting ornaments or arranging garlands.

As if to distract herself from the itch to take over Christmas again, Ali decided to bake when she got home. Baking wasn't role-specific, Tommy liked to spend time in the kitchen too. She needed somewhere to channel her energy. Plus, the kids loved it when she made cookies.

Later that evening, Ali's eyes darted to the sugar cookies cooling on the counter as she stirred the spaghetti sauce for dinner. Pierce sat at the kitchen table, eyeing a cookie, his demeanor relaxed by the familiar routine. He leaned back in his chair, a grin spreading across his face as he eyed his mom, who seemed unusually distracted.

"How's it going with the switch?" Pierce asked, breaking the silence.

Ali paused, a smile tugging at the corner of her lips. "It's... interesting."

Pierce snorted, shaking his head. "You guys are crazy for switching. Dad's stressing about a classroom party, and you just seem lost. Honestly, I think he might actually be in worse shape than you."

She laughed, "Yeah, I think he's figuring that out the hard way."

Ali walked over to her oldest son, hugging his shoulders, "We're meeting Rachel at ten on Saturday morning."

Pierce gave her a blank expression, his shoulders slumping dramatically, "Saturday?"

"The Christmas Market," Ali reminded him.

He rolled his eyes, but a smirk tugged at the corners of his mouth. "Again, Mom?"

Ali smiled, watching her son. "It's our tradition; how about you indulge in the food trucks while I walk around with Rachel?"

Pierce's eyes lit up. "Now you're talking. Deal. But no more trees, promise?"

"Promise," Ali said, chuckling as he leaned back into his seat, looking more at ease.

As she was about to make a batch of cookie icing, Ali's gaze shifted to the kitchen counter, where she noticed the empty vanilla extract bottle. She never forgot ingredients;

being organized was one of the things she prided herself on, and she always prepared. But now, with Christmas approaching and her lack of control, she was starting to feel a little off balance.

"Hey, Pierce," she said, trying to sound casual despite the flutter in her chest. "Could you run to the store for me? I'm out of vanilla extract."

Pierce gave her a skeptical look. "You know I'm not allowed to drive alone at night yet."

Ali hesitated, Pierce had just gotten his license a month ago, and his parents had a rule about him not driving at night alone for three months. "I know, but I can't leave in the middle of making the cookies and dinner. Please, just run in and grab it."

Pierce, taking advantage of this new freedom, grabbed his keys, kissed his mom on the forehead, and walked out the door. Ali felt a strange mix of relief and anxiety settle over her.

After Pierce left, Ali began humming softly, rolling out the dough for a second batch of cookies. The house smelled like cinnamon, a scent that brought a rush of holiday nostalgia. Noah walked into the room, his excitement over cookies making him dance and sing around the kitchen, using a mixing spoon like a microphone. It wasn't long before Ali grabbed a spoon, and soon they were both laughing and singing along to the music on the radio, "Santa Claus is Coming to Town". The sound of off-key singing and the clatter of spoons hitting the counters in a perfect, messy rhythm sparked Maddie's curiosity.

She entered the room, rolling her eyes like a typical teenager, not planning to engage in these childish games. But when Ali handed her a spoon, Maddie couldn't resist. Soon, they were all having a blast. For a moment, the weight of everything, the holiday chaos, and the worry over the Christmas switch vanished.

But the fun was short-lived. As they danced and laughed, Ali's phone buzzed in her pocket, and a number she did not recognize appeared on the screen.

She answered it on the second ring. "Hello?"

"Mrs. Crawford?" The voice on the other end was calm, too calm. "This is Officer Hernandez from the police department. I'm afraid your son Pierce has been in an accident. He appears to be okay, but we're taking him to the hospital to get checked out."

Ali's heart lurched as she stepped into the family room to take the call. "Is he hurt? What happened?"

"He's alert and conscious. No major injuries, but we're being cautious. Please meet us at the hospital."

The room seemed to spin around her. Maddie and Noah were still dancing, oblivious to the gravity of the situation. Ali's voice wavered as she forced herself to appear calm, "Maddie, stay here with Noah," she said quickly. "I'll be back."

Without waiting for a response, Ali rushed out the door, the frantic beat of her heart echoing in her chest. She didn't tell the kids where she was going. All she could think about was getting to Pierce, now.

CHAPTER 7

Tommy

While Ali was rushing to the hospital, Tommy was at the radio station, helping Luis with a special segment for their holiday food drive. The station was bustling with volunteers sorting canned goods into neatly labeled boxes, the hum of Christmas music weaving through the chatter. The annual drive had always been one of Tommy's favorite events. It was a reminder that the holidays weren't just about lights and presents—they were about people, too.

Luis leaned into the mic, his signature charm in full force. "If you're just tuning in, we're live from the KZ95 Holiday Food Drive! Swing by, drop off some non-perishables, and help us make this season brighter for families in need." He glanced over at Tommy and gave him a thumbs-up.

Tommy returned the gesture, but his mind felt scattered. Something was off. It wasn't any one thing he could put his finger on, just a nagging sense that the day wasn't unfolding as planned. He shook his head, trying to focus.

The sense of unease lingered. Tommy tried to brush it off as holiday stress. After all, he was juggling work, the kids, and his ever-growing Christmas to-do list. Maybe his brain was just fried.

By the time he left the station, it was late, and the sharp December air nipped at his face. He climbed into his car, cranked up the heat, and turned on the radio. Luis's voice filled the car, cheerful and steady, but it only made the unease gnaw at him more.

Pulling into the driveway, he noticed the house was still dark, except for the faint glow from the living room window. That was odd. Both Ali's and Pierce's cars were missing. Usually, the house was lit up, the sound of the kids' laughter spilling out even before he opened the door. Tonight, it felt unnervingly still.

Inside, Maddie and Noah were sitting on the couch, unusually subdued. Noah was clutching a stuffed animal, Maddie's face solemn.

"Where's your mom?" Tommy asked, shrugging off his coat.

Maddie hesitated. "She—uh—she had to go out."

"Go out? Where?"

Maddie shifted nervously, glancing at Noah. "I don't know... she rushed out about an hour ago. She seemed worried."

Tommy froze, his stomach dropping as every nerve in his body went on high alert. This was extremely abnormal. Ali rushing out without leaving word wasn't like her at all.

His heart pounded as he pulled out his phone and dialed Ali's number. It went straight to voicemail.

"Okay, okay," he muttered to himself, pacing the kitchen. On the counter, a half-completed dinner sat untouched, and a tray of unfrosted cookies rested nearby, abandoned mid-task.

Tommy gripped the edge of the counter, trying to steady himself. That feeling he'd been trying to shake all evening. It wasn't nothing.

Something was wrong.

CHAPTER 8

Ali

Ali sat in the stiff hospital chair, staring at the white bandage on Pierce's arm. A faint purple bruise was forming just below it. Nothing serious, the doctor had reassured her, just minor injuries. But her heart still hadn't stopped pounding.

Pierce sat next to her, his head hung low. He was holding a Styrofoam cup of water, twisting it in his hands. The soft murmur of voices from other rooms drifted through the hall, but Ali couldn't focus on anything except the boy in front of her.

Her boy.

He could have been seriously hurt—or worse. And it was her fault.

"Mom, I'm sorry," Pierce said quietly, breaking the silence. His voice wavered, thick with guilt. "I didn't see the car when I turned. I swear, I looked, but it just—"

"Shh," Ali reached out, placing a hand over his. She didn't want him to relive it, not now. "We're okay. You're okay. That's what matters."

Pierce nodded but didn't look up.

The nurse came in briefly to hand over discharge papers, giving Ali a sympathetic smile before leaving. As soon as the door clicked shut, Ali exhaled, her chest tightening again. She wasn't just worried about Pierce. She also had to figure out what to tell Tommy.

Pierce should not have been driving alone at night. They both knew it. The agreement had always been clear: no solo driving after dark, not until he had more experience. But she had let it slide tonight because it benefited her. It was selfish and irresponsible to send him out. Tommy would lose his mind when he found out.

"Mom?" Pierce's voice pulled her back. He finally looked up, his brown eyes full of regret. "What are we going to tell Dad?"

Ali pressed her fingers to her temples. She could feel a headache building, the stress pressing down on her like a weight.

"We'll tell him you had car trouble this afternoon," she said after a long pause, her voice low.

"Car trouble?"

"Just for tonight," she added quickly. "We'll figure out the rest later. I just... I can't deal with this right now."

Pierce looked hesitant but nodded. "I get it."

Ali hated herself a little for even suggesting it. Honesty was something she'd always tried to teach her kids. But she couldn't bear the thought of Tommy's reaction, not tonight, when the weight of the mistake already felt unbearable.

Pierce, his voice sounding small said, "I am really sorry, Mom."

"I know, honey," she said, pulling him into a hug and blinking back tears.

When they got home, Ali would have to face Tommy. And sooner or later, the truth. But tonight, she would let Pierce's "car trouble" be the only explanation. The bruises on his arm were hidden beneath the sleeves of his sweatshirt, something Tommy wouldn't notice yet.

CHAPTER 9

Tommy

Tommy had not slept well the night before. Even after Ali and Pierce had arrived home, safe and sound, something still felt off. Ali's explanation about car trouble didn't sit right with him; it was vague and uncharacteristic of her detailed personality. But he'd been too relieved to push for details, choosing instead to hold onto the sight of Pierce walking through the door, seemingly unharmed.

As he settled into his office on Friday morning, he glanced at the calendar on the wall, doing the same mental math Ali had done a week prior. Twenty-two days until Christmas. He needed every last one of them to survive this self-inflicted holiday marathon, but at the same time, he wished it would all just be over.

Luis poked his head into the office, a toothy, jolly grin on his face. "Cookies are covered," he announced like a man who had just solved world hunger. "Two dozen gluten-filled, sugar-coated Christmas creations, two dozen Jewish Hamantaschen, and one dozen gluten-free... something." He shrugged. "They'll be ready by next Friday for the party."

Tommy let out a breath of relief, leaning back in his chair. "Tell your cousin she's a lifesaver," he said, feeling the weight lift off his shoulders for exactly five seconds. He had started a to-do list, and this was the first thing he could check off. The list was hidden in a document on his phone under the title "groceries," just in case Ali got suspicious and decided to peek. She didn't need to know how far off the deep end he was diving.

Next up: the arts and crafts project. Tommy pulled out his phone and typed *diorama* into the search bar. The word felt like something from a distant, forgotten childhood, like recess or long summer afternoons. Did kids even do dioramas anymore?

Diorama: *a replica of a scene, typically a three-dimensional model, either full-sized or miniature. Sometimes enclosed in a glass showcase for museums.*

Great. Tommy wondered for a second if he could repurpose the old fish tank in the garage. A class diorama inside a fish tank? It was a stroke of genius—or at least, a desperate idea he could sell as creative. But the logistics of hauling that thing to Noah's classroom were enough to crush that dream before it even started. With a sigh, he turned to Google, knowing that if he was going to survive this, he needed the internet on his side. One hour and many questionable DIY links later, he had put together a plan. Legos for some students to build houses. Green pipe cleaners and mini pom-poms for Christmas trees, thanks to a YouTube tutorial. And because no Christmas village diorama was complete without it, a kit to make fake snow. It was ambitious for him, but at this point, Tommy felt like he was already in over his head, so why not? There were eighteen students in Noah's class; they would divide and conquer. Surely some of them knew how to work with Legos, right? He took a deep breath. He was terrified, but he was pushing through. Forget getting any actual work done today; he was now fully immersed in the world of dioramas, pipe cleaners, and fake snow.

Next on the list: Hanukkah decorations. Tommy pulled up Amazon and quickly added a menorah, some dreidels, and a pack of blue-and-white streamers to his cart. He clicked "buy now" and sat back, feeling a small victory course through him.

But there was something else weighing on him, something bigger than cookies, menorahs, or dioramas. Yesterday, he stopped by the church during his lunch break and picked an angel tree recipient. Unlike most people who grabbed tags for toddlers or young kids, because, let's face it, who doesn't love shopping for toys, he had chosen a 14-year-old boy. Tommy's heart tugged at the thought that older kids might not get picked as often, and the last thing he wanted was for someone to be left out.

His plan was set. Sunday afternoon, he would take the whole family to the mall to shop for the boy's gifts. The kids could see Santa while they were there. Ali usually made a big deal out of booking an experience with Santa months in advance, but Tommy was determined to do this his way, efficiently. No reservations, no overplanning. Just a quick stop at the food court, grab the gifts, and snap a few photos with Santa. In and out.

As Tommy glanced at his phone again, pulling up his checklist, he felt a slight pang of anxiety, but also determination. He had already handled things his way, and this angel tree shopping trip was going to be no different. Maybe Ali would have scheduled an elaborate outing, but this wasn't her Christmas to run.

☑ Cookies Ordered – Check.

☑ Diorama Supplies Ordered – Check.

☑ Hanukkah Decorations from Amazon – Check.

☑ Angel Tree Shopping Plan – Set for Sunday.

By the time Tommy pulled into the driveway Friday evening, the first thing he noticed was that their house stood out for all the wrong reasons. The neighbors had clearly gone all out this year. Twinkling lights framed every window, trees were aglow in front yards, inflatable reindeer bobbed cheerfully in the breeze, and there was even a house with a full-on synchronized light show to holiday music. It was as if the entire block had entered a competition that Tommy had somehow missed. And then there was the Crawford house, which sat in the pitch dark. It looked like it had been skipped over by Christmas itself, except for a single snowflake wreath Tommy had found in a bin labeled "old decorations," and had decided to revisit.

He shut the car door and stared at the house for a moment, his lips twitching into a grin. This was Ali's department. They had agreed that she was in charge of the outside decorations while he handled the indoor decorating. Ali had fallen behind on her duties. Tommy grabbed his bag and headed inside, already rehearsing how he would bring it up.

Inside, the scene was the usual Crawford evening mix of mild commotion. Noah was annoying Maddie, running after her and shrieking. At the same time, Pierce who was stretched out on the couch, with the remote in hand, had his attention completely stolen by a documentary on Netflix about NFL football players and their lives on and off the field.

Ali was at the kitchen counter with a glass of wine as she flipped through her latest copy of *Southern Living*. Tommy slid up next to her and gave her a side-eye glance.

"Hey, hon," he began, trying to sound casual, "did you happen to notice that we're the only house on the block without Christmas lights?"

Ali looked up from her magazine, raising an eyebrow. "Oh, don't start. I know, okay? I have a plan."

"Hey, no judgment!" Tommy held up his hands defensively. "I just thought it was part of the deal that you were handling outside." Proud of his recent accomplishments, he bragged, "I have already ordered enough supplies to turn Noah's classroom into a holiday wonderland, but... our house? It's looking a bit more like the Grinch lives here."

Ali let out a sigh, rubbing her forehead. "I know, I know. I'll get to it." She had been avoiding this task because she did not know where to start, but she needed to figure it out and soon.

Tommy wrapped an arm around her shoulders. She was in for a hard job with those outside lights. He did not envy her one bit, but he was not about to say that. It was better to keep things light. Changing the subject, Tommy asked, "How about Thai food for dinner?"

Ali's face softened. "Thai sounds amazing."

"Good," Tommy said, grabbing his phone. "I'll even place the order."

By the time the food arrived, the whole family had gathered around the table. As they dug into papaya salad and pad Thai, Tommy could not help but look around at the chaos of their house including an undecorated tree that somehow looked lopsided in the corner with no presents. He had not even started to shop for gifts yet.

But for the first time in a long week, he wasn't stressed about it. Between ordering takeout, cracking jokes with Ali, and getting a little bit of holiday planning done, it felt like maybe, just maybe, he was starting to figure this whole Christmas thing out.

"Okay," he said, raising his fork for a toast. "To surviving Christmas, one day at a time."

Ali laughed, clinking her fork against his. "Cheers to that."

And just like that, the Crawfords settled into their evening, surrounded by to-go boxes and good-natured banter, ready to face whatever holiday chaos came their way next. Lights or no lights, they were in this together. And Sunday, they'd tackle their angel tree shopping, with a side of Santa.

CHAPTER 10

Ali

Early Saturday morning, Ali stood at the kitchen counter, eyeing the mess of tangled Christmas lights she had pulled from the storage bin. "Why did I agree to this?" she mumbled to herself, running a hand through her hair. Tommy had taken over decorating the inside of the house this year, so the outside was her responsibility. She had woken up optimistic after a much-needed enjoyable night with her family, thinking she could manage stringing lights along the roof. But now, staring at the knot of wires, her confidence was slipping.

For a fleeting moment, she considered hiring someone to do the lights. It would be easy enough to call a professional, hand over the problem, and let them deal with it. But she could not take the easy way out, not this time. She had been throwing money at her problems since the switch began, and while it had solved a few headaches, it was not the real solution.

Ali sighed, grabbing a strand of lights, and beginning the tedious work of untangling them. This was her mess to fix, and she was not going to back out now.

Her phone buzzed, reminding her about plans with Rachel that morning. "Christmas Farmer's Market, Downtown, Saturday," the calendar notification chirped. Ali sighed. She had promised Rachel, she would join her, but she still planned to keep her wallet closed. However, resisting the festive stalls might be harder than she had anticipated.

At breakfast, Pierce wandered into the kitchen. "Are we still going to the market this morning?" he asked, already eyeing his mom's purse on the table.

Ali smiled knowingly. "Yes, and all the food trucks will be waiting for you."

By 10:30 am, the three of them were at the downtown market, weaving through a maze of vendor booths and twinkling string lights. Ali marveled at the rows of handmade crafts, warm cider stands, and booths overflowing with ornaments. She fought the urge to stop at every stall, repeating her promise to herself: *I am not buying anything.*

Rachel nudged her with a grin. "You're looking tempted already."

"I'm fine," Ali insisted, but her eyes betrayed her, lingering on a little wooden ornament shaped like a Christmas tree. She shook her head, pulling herself away. "I promised."

Rachel smirked.

As the morning went on, Ali's resistance began to wane. They approached a stall full of ornaments, each one more whimsical than the last. One in particular caught her eye, a small wooden heart with an inscription that read: *Family, a little bit of crazy and a whole lot of love.* She chuckled, instantly thinking of Tommy and this switch they made.

Without hesitation, she bought it.

"Okay," Rachel teased, "so much for not buying anything."

Ali waved her hand. "It's a gift for Tommy. I'll let myself off the hook for this one."

Ali watched as Rachel disappeared into a booth overflowing with handmade jewelry, her face lighting up with excitement. Ali wandered away and decided to give her friend the space to shop at her leisure. Usually, she would dive into the market alongside Rachel, combing through every booth for hidden treasures. But this year was different.

Her gaze shifted to Pierce, and she joined him near the food trucks. He was biting into what had to be the largest corn dog she had ever seen. A laugh escaped her as she made her way over. "Hungry?" she teased, nudging his shoulder.

Pierce grinned, a smear of mustard at the corner of his mouth. "You have to try this, Mom. It's life-changing."

"I think I'll stick to coffee," she said, stepping up to a nearby stand for a peppermint latte. With her drink in hand, the two of them wandered through the market, the festive atmosphere all around them.

Live music floated through the air as a local band played a jazzy rendition of "Jingle Bells." Further down, the elementary school choir crowded onto a small stage, their young voices cheerfully belting out "Here Comes Santa Claus." Ali stopped in her tracks, smiling as Pierce slowed beside her. She could not help but feel a swell of nostalgia as she listened, imagining when Maddie was up there a few years prior.

As they strolled, Ali realized how rare it was to have one-on-one time with Pierce. She would not have this moment if she had stayed with Rachel, engrossed in her usual shopping routine.

They clapped along with the crowd as the song ended, and Ali turned to Pierce. "You ready for more food, or are you full yet?"

Pierce smirked. "What do you think?" He led her back toward the food trucks, making a beeline for a truck selling funnel cakes. A few minutes later, he emerged with the sugary treat piled high with powdered sugar. They found an empty picnic table and sat down to share it, tearing off pieces of the still-warm dough.

As they ate, Ali took a deep breath. The moment was light and carefree, but the weight of the accident pressed on her. She glanced at Pierce, who was focused on his next bite.

"We need to talk," she said gently.

Pierce's chewing slowed, and he looked at her, a trace

of nervousness in his expression.

"I've been thinking about the accident," Ali continued. "I can't keep this from Dad. It's not who we are as a family to keep secrets. He deserves to know the truth."

Pierce hesitated, brushing sugar from his fingers. "I know," he said after a moment. "I just... I hate that he'll know I messed up."

Ali reached over and placed a hand on his. "I am the one who messed up, honey. I asked you to drive at night, and I didn't tell the complete truth when we got home. But honesty is what matters now. We'll tell him together, okay?"

Pierce nodded, the tension in his shoulders easing. "Okay."

As they finished the funnel cake, Ali looked at her son, grateful for this unexpected time with him. She had spent the week wrapped up in stress and worry, but today reminded her of what mattered, moments like this, the unplanned fun.

Later that afternoon, as Ali and Pierce walked through the door, Tommy's voice cut through the air like a blade. "Ali!"

She froze, the grocery bag slipping slightly in her hand. Tommy barged into the entryway, his face red with anger.

"I just got off the phone with the hospital," he said, his voice trembling. "They had a question about our insurance and informed me there was an accident."

Ali's heart sank. She glanced at Pierce, who shrank back toward the stairs, before meeting Tommy's furious gaze. "Tommy, I was going to tell you—"

"Going to tell me?" he snapped. "When Ali? After the holidays? Next week? I should have been told the second it happened. He's *our son*! And you lied to me."

"I know," she said quickly, her voice breaking. "You're right. I should have told you."

Tommy, not able to compose himself, threw his hands up and yelled, "Do you know how lucky we are that he wasn't hurt worse? That he didn't hurt someone else? This isn't something you hide."

Ali felt tears prick her eyes, guilt washing over her like a tidal wave. "I made a mistake. I handled it wrong." She took a shaky breath, trying to quickly explain. "It was his first time driving alone at night. He pulled out of the grocery store parking lot and took a right as a car approached in the left lane. The headlights were so close that it spooked him. He overcorrected and hit a street sign. No one else was involved, thank God. He has a couple of bruises on his arm, but he's okay." She looked at Tommy, her voice cracking. "I should've told you right away."

Tommy ran a hand through his hair, his frustration palpable. He glanced at Pierce, who lingered silently on the stairs. "We'll talk more later," he said, his tone sharp. "But this isn't over."

Pierce nodded, avoiding eye contact, and Tommy turned back to Ali. "I need some space," he said firmly before retreating to the back porch to cool off.

Ali exhaled shakily, feeling the weight of his disappointment settle over her like a heavy blanket.

Trying to shake off the tension, she headed outside

with Maddie a short while later. Her daughter stared at the bins of Christmas decorations, arms crossed and a small frown on her face.

"Do you want help with the Christmas lights, Mom?" Maddie asked, her tone soft and sympathetic.

Ali sighed, her smile faint. "Sure. Let's at least get them out of the box."

They pulled out the bins together, Maddie carefully inspecting each strand while Ali tried to focus. The chaos in her mind was mirrored in the mess of tangled lights.

Maddie worked quietly, her small hands picking through the knots with surprising patience. She held up a fully untangled strand of lights. "I think I'm good at this."

Ali stared at her in amazement. "I'm hiring you every year."

Maddie smiled. Together, they sorted through the rest of the lights, and while Ali knew the real work was still ahead, she felt a little lighter with Maddie by her side.

On Sunday morning, Ali woke up early, determined to get the lights hung before she chickened out. She dragged the ladder from the garage, coffee in hand, and stared at the roofline. It was higher than she remembered. After a deep breath, she climbed up, light strands in tow.

It did not take long for the frustration to set in. The lights kept slipping. Every time she thought she had a section secured, it fell right back down. After the third time of climbing up and down the ladder, her patience was thinning.

"Why won't you stay!" she growled, glaring at the row of hooks that were supposed to hold the lights in place.

From below, Maddie appeared, peeking up at her. "Need more help, Mom?"

Ali sighed, hands on her hips. "You wouldn't happen to know a magic trick for making these things stay, would you?"

Maddie laughed. "No, but I can hand you the lights so you don't have to climb up and down."

Ali smiled despite her frustration. "Deal."

With Maddie's help, she managed to string a few more sections, but the stubborn lights still had a mind of their own. Ali was sure half the neighborhood could hear her muttering under her breath, fighting with every tangle and misplaced bulb.

Just as they were making progress, Tommy appeared at the base of the ladder, looking up at them with a hard edge in his eyes.

"Hey," he said, his voice flat. "I'm taking the kids to the mall."

Ali stopped focusing on the strand currently giving her trouble, the tone in his voice cutting through her. She glanced down at him. "Now?"

"Yes, I'm taking them to shop for the angel tree gifts," Tommy replied, his hands shoved deep in his pockets. His gaze was firm, obviously still upset. "We'll pick up gifts, grab a snack at the food court, and the kids can see Santa."

Ali's brow furrowed, irritation rising in her chest. "Santa? Tommy, I can't just stop now. I'm making progress with these lights."

He didn't flinch. "You're finally making progress? You've been at it all morning. I'm doing this now. It's on you if you want to join."

The words stung more than she expected. She tried to hold his gaze but found herself looking away instead. "I'm not just going to drop everything."

Tommy's tone didn't soften. "Fine, don't. But I'm not waiting around. You've got your lights, and I've got the kids."

He turned to leave without another word, his back to her, making it clear the decision had already been made. Ali couldn't help but think he was punishing her for excluding him the other night when she received the call about the accident.

Ali's heart sank at the thought of missing out on the family outing, but she felt stuck by the pressure of getting this job done. She called out to him, "I just... I need to finish this. It's important to me."

Tommy nodded as he walked into the house, "I get it."

He gathered the kids, including her light-hanging partner, Maddie, and within minutes, they were bundled up and ready to go. Ali watched as they piled into the car, her stomach knotting with guilt as they drove off without her.

She picked up the tangled strand of lights, but the spark had dimmed. The joy she'd felt at finally making progress had been replaced by a hollow ache.

Ali glanced at her watch as she cleaned up later that evening—nine hours. Nine hours of fighting with lights that refused to cooperate. She had not even started to decorate the mailbox or put out the nutcrackers that usually stood proudly outside the front door, greeting holiday visitors. Crooked, falling-down lights were all she had to show for her day's inexperienced effort. She was discouraged but also too exhausted to care.

As Ali stepped inside, she was immediately hit with the comforting smell of Tommy's homemade chili. Typically, the scent of simmering spices and warm cornbread would have melted away the frustrations of the day. But today, the heaviness in her chest lingered.

Tommy was already ladling chili into bowls, his expression hard to read. The kids had scattered to the living room, leaving the two of them in an uncomfortable silence.

She eyed the mismatched and messy tree and sighed, slumping into her chair at the table. The big Christmas tree that usually sat in the family room with its carefully coordinated ornaments was...different. She squinted at it, taking in the sight. All the ornaments from the kids' tree in the playroom hung on it. There was no rhyme or reason, just a jumble of colorful decorations—handmade, glitter-covered, chipped edges, and all. Someone had raided the "sentimental" box. Her eyes landed on the tree skirt next. The once-white fabric still bore the infamous punch stain from a few Christmases ago, when her 5-year-old niece, Claire, 4-year-old Noah, and her sister's cat were left unsupervised in the family room for just two minutes. To this day, she was still unsure what exactly had happened. Ali had meant to throw that thing out. Why hadn't she? Now it sat under the tree, slightly lopsided, its faded pink stain peeking out from the folds.

Ali took it all in—the uncoordinated ornaments, including a broken red bulb lying on the ground barely detectable in the disorder, the crooked, stained tree skirt, and the chili simmering on the stove. She let out a deep sigh.

Focusing back on Tommy, she asked, "When did you get a chance to make this?" realizing she had barely stepped foot in the house all day. She didn't know Tommy had prepared chili; she'd missed the outing with her family and missed the kids decorating the tree.

Tommy slid her a bowl. "Before I took the kids shopping, so it could simmer while we were gone."

"How was the mall?" she asked, not quite ready to talk about the accident again or the mess of lights still taunting her outside.

Tommy shrugged, "The kids had fun shopping. Santa pictures didn't turn out so great. Santa wasn't very festive."

Ali paused, her spoon mid-air. "I would've taken them somewhere better."

It was out before she could stop herself. The words hung between them, sharp and biting. Tommy's hand stilled as he set down the cornbread. He did not look at her, but she could see the tension in his shoulders.

"I'm sorry," she muttered, immediately regretting it. "That came out wrong."

Tommy finally met her gaze, his jaw tight. "You think I don't know that? I did what I could today, Ali. You weren't there."

Guilt tugged at her stomach again. She knew she had missed something important, and the way Tommy said it, the weight in his voice, made it worse.

She pushed her food around with her spoon, her appetite fading. "I know I wasn't. I just... I wanted to get the lights done, and now I'm not even happy with how they look."

They sat in silence for a few beats, the only sounds were the clinking of spoons against bowls. The chili, as always, was delicious, but it did little to soothe the tension hanging in the air.

Finally, Tommy spoke, his voice softer now. "I'm going to take a shower and call it an early night."

Ali's shoulders fell as she nodded. They both knew the weekend had not gone as planned, and neither of them was completely innocent in how it had unraveled.

That night while trying to fall asleep knowing they hadn't resolved a thing, the bed felt cold to Ali despite Tommy lying next to her, both of them too tired and too frustrated to make amends.

CHAPTER 11

Tommy

Wednesday morning, Tommy sat at the kitchen table, staring at the calendar on his phone. Two days until Noah's classroom holiday party, and he was feeling... almost ready. The gluten-free cookies were covered, the Hanukkah decorations had arrived, and the arts-and-crafts supplies were set to be delivered tomorrow. He checked his list one more time, nodding in satisfaction.

But his sense of accomplishment was fleeting. He glanced at the gift list on his phone. Other than the Angel Tree gifts, he had not bought a single present yet. His stomach knotted slightly as he thought about all the people he still needed gifts for—Ali, the kids, his parents, Ali's parents, not to mention the teachers, friends, and neighbors.

As he sat there, something more important was on his mind. He hated how things had been with Ali lately, how tense and disconnected they felt. They were not fighting exactly, but there had been this unspoken unease ever since he found out about the accident. The robotic movements each day going through their routine, the half-hearted conversations, it all just felt off. He wasn't used to this kind of rift with Ali. Sure, they had disagreements, but they usually found their way back to normal quickly.

This time, though, it had taken days for things to thaw. The quiet resentment they both carried had settled like a fog over the house. It wasn't until yesterday that they started talking again, and even then, it was more functional than affectionate. This morning felt different, lighter and easier. They were talking more, and it seemed like the stiffness was finally breaking.

Ali walked into the kitchen, hesitating at the doorway, unsure how to approach him. "Hey," he said, breaking the tension. "Can we talk?"

Ali leaned against the doorframe; arms crossed. "Sure."

He laid down his phone, then turned to face her fully. There was a softness in his eyes now, a gentleness that had been missing for days. "I was thinking… maybe we should go on a date tonight. Clear the air."

Ali didn't respond immediately.

Tommy's voice cut through her thoughts, his expression more vulnerable now. "I'm not good at holding grudges. I don't like feeling distant from you. I don't know how everything got so out of hand."

Ali pushed herself off the doorframe and moved closer to him, "I don't like it either, Tommy"

"I know," he said, his voice low. "I miss you."

Ali smiled softly, her tension easing at his words. "Okay. A date it is."

Tommy's face broke into a small grin. "Great. I'll make reservations." Maybe they were on the mend, and Tommy felt enormous relief at the thought.

Later that afternoon, Tommy sat at his desk, staring at a stack of Christmas cards in front of him instead of his usual paperwork. His hand was cramping, and his tongue felt like he'd been eating cotton balls from licking envelopes for the past hour. What had seemed like a small task had taken hours. All he wanted was to get these cards in the mail and be done with it.

He had completed a little over half of them. His neck was stiff from hunching over, and his fingers were numb. Glancing at the clock, he realized he had just enough time to get to the post office before they closed. But as he looked at the stack of remaining cards, something inside him shifted.

He was chasing perfection; the cards, meant to be a simple tradition, had become a small mountain of stress.

With a deep breath, Tommy pushed the remaining cards to the side. He wasn't going to finish them, and that was okay. It was Christmas, his way. He grabbed the stack of completed cards, still not perfect but close enough, and tossed them in his bag.

"I'm done," he muttered to himself, a small smile tugging at his lips.

The thought felt liberating. Next year he would help Ali get all the cards done, but this year, he was calling it quits.

Tommy bolted out of the office, running across the parking lot. After what felt like a race against time, he barely made it to the post office before the doors closed. The clerk gave him a sympathetic look as he slid the cards across the counter. Tommy exhaled, feeling lighter than he had in days.

Done.

On the drive home to pick up Ali for their date, his phone rang. It was Skip's wife, Mary-Anne.

"Hey, Tommy!" she chirped. "Just wanted to touch base about the Christmas party with the neighborhood crew. We're still on for next Saturday, right?"

Tommy's heart sank as he remembered the neighborhood Christmas party. The date had been on the calendar for months, but with the madness of switching roles with Ali, he had completely forgotten about it.

"Uh, yeah! Of course!" he stammered, trying to sound like he had everything under control. "Just finalizing the details."

"Great," Mary-Anne replied, though Tommy could hear the hesitation in her voice. "So, what's the plan this year? Usually, Ali organizes the food, drinks, and the gift exchange. Have you got all that sorted?"

Tommy's brain scrambled for an answer. "Well, the food... I'm working on that. And gift exchange... um..." His voice trailed off, the panic rising in his chest. He had not even thought about a gift exchange. The same question had started popping up in his mind daily, How did Ali keep all this straight?

There was a brief pause on the other end of the line, and Tommy could tell Mary-Anne had picked up on his floundering.

"Tell you what," she said kindly. "I'll reach out to our friends and coordinate the gift exchange and appetizers. You've got enough on your plate. If you can handle the main course, that'd be great."

Tommy exhaled slowly. "That would be a huge help. Thanks, Mary-Anne." He ran a hand through his hair, grateful for the lifeline.

"No problem," she replied.

Tommy could almost see Ali rolling her eyes at him if she knew how much he was winging it.

"And Ali usually makes a specialty cocktail and has champagne for the toast," Mary-Anne added.

"Yep, specialty cocktail, champagne. I'll make sure to pick those up," Tommy said, making a mental note. "Everyone usually brings sodas, beer, and wine, right?" He asked vaguely remembering that part from previous years.

"Exactly!" Mary-Anne's voice brightened. "It's always a group effort, but Ali really does make it all happen, doesn't she?"

Tommy chuckled, though the truth of that statement stung a little. "Yeah, she's... pretty amazing at it all."

"Well, don't worry, Tommy. We've got your back. I'll touch base with everyone. You just focus on the main course and the specialty drink," Mary-Anne sounded so confident that they could pull it off, Tommy wished he felt the same way.

After they hung up, Tommy slumped in his seat. One more thing added to the list: Noah's party, the Christmas gifts, and the neighborhood party. Ali made all of this look so easy, but now that it was on him. Tommy felt like he was close to drowning, barely keeping his head above water.

Tommy walked through the door, tossing his keys on the counter. The house smelled like the tacos that Ali was making for the kids for dinner. He found her in the kitchen, still in her work clothes, wiping her hands on a towel, she looked up at him, and for the first time in a while, there was no immediate tension between them. Just…quiet.

"Kids are all set," Ali said. "I just need 10 minutes to freshen up."

He nodded, running a hand through his hair. "Okay," the silent lull between them still hanging in the air.

The drive to The Wash House, Ali's favorite restaurant, was quiet. He could feel her next to him, but it wasn't the comfortable silence that usually came when they were together. No, this one felt heavier. Still, he was relieved that at least they were doing something together, getting out of the house. That was a start.

They parked and walked inside, the familiar hum of conversation and clinking glasses greeting them. The hostess smiled as they were led to their table by the window. After Ali sat, she picked up the menu, but Tommy didn't bother. He knew what he was having, the filet medium-rare, with a side of his favorite dish at the restaurant, truffled-gouda mashed potatoes.

The waiter came over, and Ali ordered a lemon drop martini. Tommy went with a beer, wanting something simple and comforting. They both ordered quickly, but once the waiter left, it was silent again. The kind of silence that wasn't comfortable or familiar.

Tommy reached for the napkin, fidgeting. But it was her words, not his, that started the conversation. She spoke first.

"I feel horrible about the accident," Ali said, her voice soft but steady. "I should've told you. I shouldn't have kept it from you, and I'm really sorry."

Her apology hung in the air. He could see how badly it bothered her, the guilt and regret etched in her face. He deserved to be angry, to stay mad about it, but seeing her like this made it impossible to hold on to that frustration.

"I'm sorry, too," Tommy said, his voice low. "I shouldn't have taken the kids shopping and to see Santa without you. It was payback, and it was petty. I should have let you be a part of it."

Ali met his gaze then, her eyes softening. She didn't say anything right away, but he knew she understood. He wasn't perfect, and she wasn't either. But that was the part of them he loved the most—the ability to mess up, to make mistakes, and still find a way back to each other.

Their drinks arrived then, interrupting the silence. The clink of the glasses being set on the table felt like a small moment of peace between them. They raised their glasses, and Tommy's heart lightened just a bit. The strain that had been hanging over them for days vanished.

Tommy didn't need any more words. He touched his glass with hers, a quiet acknowledgment that this rough patch was behind them, that they could start over, take a breath, and keep moving forward. The rest of the evening was quieter still, but not in the way it had been before. It felt more like the silence of two people finding their rhythm again.

After they arrived home, Tommy lingered downstairs, cleaning up the taco remnants his kids had left behind. He glanced over at the kitchen counter, where Ali's phone sat, likely filled with meticulous plans from past years. He wondered if just a quick look could help him figure out how to organize the party without completely dropping the ball.

He reached for the phone but stopped himself, feeling a pang of guilt. Ali had trusted him with Christmas this year and snooping through her plans felt like admitting defeat.

As the clock ticked closer to bedtime, Tommy's anxiety increased. There was still time to pull everything together, but the pressure was building.

In bed that night, Tommy tossed and turned. Every time he thought he was close to drifting off, another Christmas task popped into his head like a flashing neon sign. Noah's party. The neighborhood party. The shopping. Christmas Eve and Christmas Day? He hadn't given either a single thought.

His usual laid-back attitude had given way to a constant buzz of stress. "Why did I think I could do this?" he muttered quietly, careful not to disturb Ali, who was peacefully asleep beside him. She had handed him the reins for Christmas, and now here he was, spiraling into panic over the mounting to-do list, feeling more overwhelmed by the minute.

He squeezed his eyes shut. If he could just make it through the next couple of days, he could deal with the rest of the list later, one event at a time. But no matter how hard he tried; his brain would not stop spinning. Sleep was impossible.

After a restless Wednesday night and an entire Thursday spent ensuring everything was ready for Noah's holiday party, Tommy finally crashed. Despite his anxiety still simmering under the surface, his sheer exhaustion overtook him, granting him some much-needed sleep.

Friday morning came faster than he expected, and Tommy was determined to be punctual. Arriving at Noah's classroom a full hour early, he walked in with bags of treats and supplies, wearing a confident grin that said, I've got this.

"Mr. Crawford, thank you so much for handling the party and lunch today!" Mrs. Marin said with a bright smile as she adjusted a stack of construction paper on the craft table.

Tommy blinked, his grin freezing. "Lunch?"

"Yes, and drinks too!" she added cheerfully before bustling off to help some kids with their math assignment.

"Lunch," he muttered to himself, his stomach sinking. "And drinks."

What Tommy didn't know, what he couldn't have known, since neither Mrs. Marin nor Ali had mentioned it, was that being in charge of the classroom party also meant coordinating lunch and drinks for the entire class.

He crouched down to Noah's level, trying to keep his cool. "I'll be right back," he said, ruffling his hair.

Tommy stepped into the hallway hiding from his mistake, "Hey, Tony," Tommy said as soon as his friend picked up. "I need a favor. A big one. How fast can you get ten pizzas to Noah's school? Like…now? And do you have gluten-free crust?"

By the time Tommy walked back into the classroom, his face was flushed, and he was trying to look nonchalant. "Pizzas and lemonade are on the way!" he announced with as much enthusiasm as he could muster.

Lunch was delayed, but thankfully, Mrs. Marin saved the day by letting the kids dive into the cookies first. Tommy was horrified at the chaos it unleashed, kids bouncing off the walls, cookie crumbs everywhere, but Noah's giggles helped him relax a little.

When the pizzas finally arrived, delivered personally by Tony from Rotolo's, Tommy felt like a hero. The kids cheered, and Noah smiled which made every ounce of stress worth it.

But the diorama project? A different story. Tommy had underestimated just how much coordination went into something like this. Within minutes, he was sprinting from table to table, handing out glue sticks, pom-poms, and Lego pieces like he was putting out fires.

"Mr. Crawford, can we have more glitter glue?" one girl asked.

"Daddy! I need help with the snow!" Noah shouted.

"Mr. Crawford, the Legos are stuck!" another kid yelled.

He had no plan, no backup, and no clue how Ali made it look so effortless. If she were here, she would have had color-coded bins, assigned parent volunteers to help with each part of the project, and a timeline for putting it all together. But he did not have any of that. What he did have was sheer determination to make it through without breaking a sweat or losing his mind.

By the time the Hanukkah decorations came out, Tommy was ready for a break. Thankfully, Mrs. Marin took the lead, explaining the menorah, dreidels, and the significance of Hanukkah traditions. Tommy just stood at the back of the room, nodding his head in agreement at Mrs. Marin's lesson.

As he tried to stay focused on the party, he could not help but notice Noah. He was laughing with his friends, his face lighting up, it was pure joy. But he also noticed the way he occasionally glanced at the door, like he was hoping someone else might walk in. Ali. Tommy's chest tightened. He knew Noah missed his mom. He was not used to his dad being the one at his school events, and truthfully, Tommy wasn't used to it either.

Still, when the party wrapped up and Noah ran up to him, throwing his arms around Tommy's waist, all the stress and self-doubt melted away. "Did you have fun, buddy?" Tommy asked, resting a hand on his back.

He looked up at him, his blue eyes sparkling. "The party was awesome, Daddy."

He laughed, ruffling his hair. "You're just saying that because we had pizza and cookies."

"Nope," he said with a grin. "It's cuz you were here."

For the first time all day, Tommy felt like he had done something right.

CHAPTER 12

Ali

Ali sat at her desk, staring blankly at the emails piling up in her inbox. Noah's Christmas party was happening right now, and she wasn't there. She always made it to the school events, but this year was different.

"Tommy's got it," she told herself for the hundredth time, but it didn't make her feel any better. She knew he was capable but missing her youngest son's party stung in a way she had not expected.

By noon, Ali could not stand it anymore. The thought of Noah in his festive Santa shirt, laughing with his friends, and her not being there was more than she could bear. Grabbing her coat, she headed out for a break and drove to a nearby park, stopping under a large tree. She picked at her sandwich, but her appetite had vanished.

As she sat quietly, alone with her thoughts, a memory from long ago surfaced, clear and vivid, as if it had been waiting all this time for her to revisit it.

She saw herself as a six-year-old, the same age as Noah, standing in the middle of the living room of her childhood home with an apron tied snugly around her tiny waist. Hands firmly planted on her hips; she surveyed her domain with an unshakable confidence.

In her mind, she wasn't just little Ali, she was Mrs. Claus, the boss of Christmas. And things were not running smoothly.

"Come on! We need more toys!" she barked, pacing in front of the couch where her makeshift workshop was set up. The elves, invisible to anyone but her, were clearly slacking off, and she wasn't having it.

A row of stuffed animals lined the couch, doubling as reindeer. She gave each one a firm inspection, occasionally pausing to hand out a baby carrot from the stash she had swiped from the kitchen. "Dasher, quit messing around!" she scolded, her voice high-pitched but full of authority.

The room glowed with twinkle lights from the family tree, casting everything in warm, golden illumination. Her six-year-old self had been so sure of her role in it all that it seemed like the holiday season itself depended on her determination and effort. Christmas felt bigger than just one day.

She smiled at the memory of her reflection in one of the red glass ornaments hanging on the tree. Even then, she had loved the sense of control, the feeling that she could create magic with her own two hands. That was her favorite part, the chance to make everything feel perfect.

The memory faded as Ali returned to the present, the sound of a bicyclist riding by snapping her back to reality. Feeling restless and distracted, she made a decision. She was leaving work early. What she needed most now was the comfort of being with her kids.

Noah was at the kitchen table when she walked through the door, coloring in a holiday-themed coloring book. His face lit up as he saw his mom.

"Noah!" Ali dropped her bag and immediately pulled her son into a tight hug. "I'm so sorry I missed your party."

He looked up at her with his big, innocent eyes. "It's okay, Mom. Daddy was there, and the pizza was so good. We ate cookies first!"

Ali smiled, but it didn't completely ease her heart. "I'll make it up to you, sweetie. I promise."

"You don't have to, Mommy," Noah reassured her. Her kind-hearted baby boy gave her a quick kiss on the cheek before wriggling free to return to his coloring.

Later that evening, Tommy was enjoying *Christmas Vacation* on television, Noah was tucked into bed, Maddie was dropped off at a sleepover, and Pierce had slipped away to hang out with friends. With the house unusually quiet and the calendar unusually open, Ali scrolled through her phone, then shot off a quick text to Rachel:

Ali: Hey, what's your night looking like?

Rachel's reply came quickly.

Rachel: Not much, just opened a bottle of wine. Want to come over?

Ali didn't hesitate.

> *Ali: Yes. I need a break.*
>
> *Rachel: I'll invite my neighbors; they're always a good time when the wine comes out. Followed by the winking smiley face emoji.*
>
> *Ali: Great, I love hanging out with them. This is exactly what I need.*

By the time Ali arrived, the warm glow of candles greeted her at the door, and Rachel's cozy living room already filled with the familiar hum of laughter and chatter. Surrounded by a few girlfriends, Ali sank into the comfort of the evening.

It did not take long for the conversation to shift from a lighthearted catch-up to the realities of juggling the holidays, and Ali found herself letting go of some of the stress she had been carrying.

"I don't know how I'm going to make it until Christmas," Ali said, taking another big sip from her glass.

Her friends laughed, but Ali just shook her head, feeling the warmth of the alcohol start to ease her worries. "Seriously," she added. "There's still so much to do."

"It's the battle with the Christmas lights, questioning Tommy's choices about the presents, the parties, and then there's this guilt about missing things like Noah's party today," she continued, her words starting to slur just a little.

"Yeah," Rachel's neighbor, Julia, chimed in. "I missed my son's Christmas play last week, and I cried the entire way home from work. You're not alone."

Ali gave her a small, comforting smile, feeling slightly better. "I guess I just like being in charge of all the holiday magic. It's who I am, a part of me."

"That's why we're here," Rachel said, raising her glass. "To get drunk and forget about all the stuff we didn't do. I have an idea, let's hit the mall and get ourselves some matching Christmas PJs. I'm thinking reindeer."

Ali burst out laughing, the tension easing even more. "I am so in."

By the time they left the store, the women were tipsy, with matching Christmas pajamas, and already half-giggling at the thought of wearing them out. They piled into the Uber after changing clothes in the restroom, doubling over in laughter as they adjusted their reindeer antlers and jingle bell socks.

From the backseat of the car, they spotted a sign outside a small, unassuming bar that read "Karaoke Tonight—Everyone Welcome!" It was the kind of place that catered to the 70+ crowd, with twinkling, colorful Christmas lights framing the entrance. Ali and Rachel exchanged a mischievous glance and asked the driver to let them out.

Inside, the bar was snug, with about twenty-five people packed inside, all at least thirty years their senior. They were greeted by a sea of gray hair and friendly, wrinkled faces. A glittering disco ball hung from the ceiling, casting shimmering lights across the room, and a hand-painted karaoke sign adorned the back wall. Tambourines were set on the tables, alongside small bells to jingle while others sang.

Their outfits, more festive than anything the regulars had seen in years, earned them stares and a round of free drinks. But the real fun started once the karaoke machine was fired up.

A man with a walker shuffled slowly toward the stage, the crowd parting for him like he was a celebrity. With a sly grin and a sparkle in his eye, he grabbed the microphone and launched into a surprisingly smooth rendition of "My Girl." As he sang, he pointed playfully at Ali and her friends, his performance half-serenade, half-comedy routine. The room erupted in laughter and applause, his charm lighting up the space.

By the time Rachel grabbed Ali's hand and pulled her on stage with the rest of their friends, tambourines in tow, the crowd was already warmed up and ready for more. Together, the group of ladies belted out a hilariously off-key rendition of "All I Want for Christmas Is You." Their exaggerated hand gestures and over-the-top dance moves earning cheers and more than a few chuckles.

As they sang, the room came alive, the older crowd jingling bells in rhythm with the music. By the end of the song, Ali's cheeks hurt from laughing, and the joy in the room felt bright. It seemed to her as though they had just put the whole room in the holiday spirit.

For the first time in days, she was not consumed by Christmas plans or regrets about what she'd missed. She was just in the moment, carefree, surrounded by friends, and letting go.

When they stumbled out of the bar hours later, still wearing their matching pajamas, Rachel looped her arm through Ali's. "That was exactly what I needed," Ali said, her cheeks flushed from both the cold and the wine.

"Same," Rachel agreed, grinning. "Next time, we wear these to the school bake sale."

Ali groaned but couldn't stop laughing. Tomorrow would bring the stress of Christmas back, but tonight? Tonight, she'd had ridiculous fun, and that was enough to keep her going.

CHAPTER 13

Tommy

Tommy had it all figured out. He'd set his alarm early on Saturday morning to beat the Christmas shopping rush so he could be home in time to join the family for the town Christmas parade that evening. A well-laid plan.

But plans, as Tommy was quickly learning this holiday season, were just opportunities for the universe to laugh in your face.

He rolled out of bed quietly, trying not to wake Ali. She was cocooned under the blankets, and Tommy wanted to give her a little extra time to sleep after last night's spontaneous holiday karaoke and pajama adventure with Rachel and the gang. He smirked to himself, still imagining them singing in those ridiculous reindeer PJs.

But his moment of amusement was short-lived as the unmistakable sound of cartoons echoed from the living room.

"Dad! I'm starving!" Noah whined as he entered the room.

Tommy groaned inward. He had been hoping to get out the door before he woke up, but no such luck. The sight that greeted him was Noah curled up on the couch, looking like he had not eaten in days, his face contorted with a frown. But worse than that, Tommy walked into the kitchen with Noah in tow, finding a small puddle forming under the kitchen sink, steadily growing as water dripped from the cabinet.

"Dad! Look!" Noah pointed to the leak; eyes wide. "The kitchen's broken!"

"Of course, it is," Tommy muttered under his breath, rubbing the back of his neck. He tossed a towel down to contain the mess, "looks like I need to grab some tools from the garage."

Noah crossed his arms. "But I'm hungry!"

"I need five minutes., I'll whip up some pancakes in a sec," Tommy countered., "Let's go grab the toolbox."

They made their way through the kitchen and out into the cool air of the garage, where the familiar scent of motor oil and dust greeted them. Tommy headed straight for the shelf where his toolbox sat, the red metal box slightly scuffed from years of use. He hoisted it off the shelf, and Noah watched in awe as if it were some treasure chest filled with mysteries.

"Think you can carry this?" Tommy teased, handing it to Noah with both hands.

Noah tried to take it from his father but quickly

gave up, shaking his head with a big smile. "No way! It's too heavy."

"Thought so," Tommy chuckled, hefting the toolbox himself and leading them inside.

Once they were back at the sink, Tommy set the box down with a metallic thud. Kneeling beside the sink, he flipped the latches open and dug through for the right wrench. Noah, crouching beside him, was wide-eyed and ready to assist.

"Can I help?" Noah asked, eager to get involved.

Tommy patted his shoulder. "Yeah, sure. Hand me that wrench over there."

Noah beamed as he passed it over, mimicking Tommy's every move, crouching just like his dad. His enthusiasm was contagious, and Tommy could not help but smile at the way Noah soaked up every moment, proud to be at his dad's side.

A few minutes later, Ali stumbled into the kitchen. Her hair was a mess, and her eyes were squinting as if the sunlight coming through the windows was personally offending her.

"Oh god... why so much noise this early?" she groaned, leaning against the counter.

"Rough morning, huh?" Tommy asked as he worked on tightening the pipe.

"Nothing two aspirin and a soda can't fix," Ali responded as she made her way to the refrigerator.

Noah turned toward her, beaming. "Mom! Me and Dad fixed the kitchen!"

"Sink was leaking, I fixed it, but keep an eye on it today," Tommy said, standing up and wiping his hands. "Now for pancakes."

Ali gave a weak thumbs-up and shuffled to the couch, where she could hide under a blanket and hope the world would quiet down until her Aspirin kicked in.

By the time Tommy managed to feed Noah and grab a quick shower, it was already mid-morning. His plan to sneak out early had evaporated, but he was determined to get his Christmas shopping done before the day completely got away from him.

"I'm heading out to do some shopping," he called over his shoulder as he grabbed his keys. "Text me if you need anything."

"Good luck," Ali called back, looking slightly more alive after breakfast and coffee.

Tommy slipped out, hoping that luck would actually be on his side. His list for the kids was straightforward: Noah wanted a remote-control dinosaur that he saw in the Christmas catalog, Maddie requested skin care products complete with pictures she had texted directly to him as a guide, and Pierce just wanted gift cards and cash to do his own shopping after Christmas.

Thirty minutes later, Tommy was standing in the middle of the toy aisle, surrounded by what could only be described as holiday shopping Armageddon. People were everywhere, frantically grabbing anything left on the shelves like it was the last lifeboat on a sinking ship.

Tommy weaved through the commotion, his eyes scanning for the dinosaur. His heart sank when he reached the aisle where the dinosaur was supposed to be. The shelf was empty. Not a single prehistoric creature in sight.

"Can I help you?" an exhausted-looking store employee asked, barely glancing up from straightening what was left on the shelves.

"Yeah, uh, I'm looking for the dinosaur action figure, the one that roars and moves?"

She gave him a pitying look. "Sold out weeks ago. You're not going to find that anywhere."

Tommy's stomach dropped. "Seriously?"

She nodded. "I could put you on a waitlist, but it wouldn't get to you before Christmas."

Tommy thanked the store clerk with a forced smile and moved on, hoping for better luck in the beauty aisle for Maddie's soap. But it was the same story in every aisle, all the popular gifts were sold out. The crowds were impossible to navigate, and he found himself jostled by frantic parents, each desperately searching for their own child's Christmas miracle.

After what felt like hours of wandering the store in defeat, Tommy left, empty-handed and frustrated. He had completely underestimated the madness of holiday shopping.

A quick glance at his phone told him the parade wasn't for a few more hours, but he was already behind schedule, and the last thing he wanted was to disappoint the kids by being late.

Before heading home, Tommy made a few more stops, scanning store shelves in a last-ditch effort to find the perfect gifts for their extended family members. With each passing stop, his frustration grew, nothing seemed right, or it was already picked over.

Sliding into the driver's seat, ready to call it a day, his phone buzzed. Seeing his mother's name on the screen, he sighed and answered, already bracing himself.

"Tommy! Pierce called us and told us about your little Christmas switcheroo," his mom said, her voice practically sparkling with excitement. "Your dad and I decided we need to see this in action. We're coming to spend Christmas with you!"

"Wait… what?" Tommy stammered, gripping the steering wheel tighter.

"We'll be there in a week," she continued, undeterred. "We can't wait to see how you're handling things. Love you, sweetie!"

The call ended before Tommy could protest, leaving him with a sinking feeling in his stomach—and a touch of betrayal toward his eldest son. The added pressure of his mom looking over his shoulder while he struggled to manage this new version of Christmas felt overwhelming. He'd need to prepare the guest room, break the news to Ali, and somehow keep everything from falling apart

As he pulled into the driveway, his stomach twisted tighter, Maddie's and Noah's gifts were still unresolved. He realized there was only one option left: the internet, acknowledging that he should have started there in the first place.

Pulling out his phone, Tommy started searching, already dreading the results. Sure enough, the dinosaur Noah wanted was now three times its original price, and the expedited shipping cost nearly made him drop his phone. Maddie's skincare set? Equally inflated. As for Pierce, he'd settled on cash—simple and foolproof.

Tommy groaned but clicked "Buy" anyway, grimacing at the dent in his wallet. The money stung, but the thought of his kids waking up disappointed on Christmas morning stung worse.

By the time he walked in the front door, Ali and the kids were ready to leave, bundled in coats and hats for the Christmas parade. Noah bounced with excitement, and even Maddie's usual teenage scowl was replaced by glowing anticipation.

"Come on, Dad!" Maddie called out, tugging on his arm.

Noah shouted while bouncing on his toes. "I want pizza!"

Tommy stopped them, holding up a finger. "First, I need to get into something a little more festive."

He dashed upstairs, pulled open his dresser, and grabbed his Christmas sweater, a goofy green-and-red knit with flashing Christmas bulb lights sewn into the fabric. Tommy grinned at his reflection in the mirror. The sweater was ridiculous, but it had become a bit of a tradition.

When he came back down, the family was already piling into the car. He joined them, the flashing lights of his sweater caused Noah to giggle and Maddie to roll her eyes as he slid into the driver's seat.

At Rotolo's, the smell of pizza hit them as soon as they walked through the door. Tony, who owned the place, was manning the front counter and waved them over with a grin.

"Hey, Tony!" Tommy called out. "Thanks again for saving me during Noah's party."

Tony laughed. "Anytime, man. We got lucky; I had that pizza dough ready. You owe me big!"

"Oh, I know it," Tommy said, rubbing the back of his neck.

As they settled at their table, the kids excitedly discussed their plans for the parade. Tommy turned to Ali, finally relaxing now that they were all together., "How was your day?" he asked while taking a sip of his IPA that came from a small brewery in Birmingham about 4 hours north of Fairhope. That first sip hit the spot after his chaotic shopping adventures earlier in the day.

Ali smiled and sighed. "I finally finished decorating the mailbox and the entryway. Took me long enough, but it's done."

Tommy's face flushed with embarrassment. He had not even noticed the decorations she'd worked so hard on. "I didn't even—" he started to say.

Ali waved it off, already moving on, "What's up? You've got that look."

He took another sip of beer for courage. "So, I talked to my mom earlier," he began, his voice hesitant.

Ali looked intrigued. "Oh? What did she say?"

"She and Dad are coming for Christmas," Tommy said, bracing himself. "Apparently, Pierce told them about the whole Christmas switch thing, and now they want to see it in action."

Ali burst into laughter. "Oh, that's amazing! Your mom's going to eat this up."

"Yeah, that's what I'm afraid of," Tommy muttered, taking a bigger gulp of his beer. "You know she's going to be watching my every move, making her little comments about how I'm doing everything wrong."

Still giggling, Ali said, "Come on, Tommy. You know she loves you. And honestly, I think it'll be hilarious. Besides, I could use a front-row seat to her teasing you about your 'Christmas skills.'"

"Great, just great," he said, shaking his head but smiling despite himself, "They'll be here in a week. So, we need to get the guest room ready."

"No problem," Ali said with a shrug. Then she paused, counting on her fingers. "Wait, how many people does that make for Christmas Day?"

Tommy groaned. "Let's see. My parents—so, two. Us and the kids—that's five. Your mom and stepdad—two more. And your sister and her family... that's four, right?"

"Yup," Ali confirmed, nodding. "So, thirteen in total."

He groaned again, closing his eyes. "Remind me why I agreed to this whole switch thing?"

"Agreed?" Ali countered. "It was your idea!"

The kids were already devouring their pizzas, oblivious to their parents' banter. Tommy leaned back, enjoying the warmth of the restaurant and the laughter of his family.

The Christmas parade in Fairhope, Alabama, a town of over 22,000 resident, was nothing short of magical, and it felt like the entire community had come out to celebrate. As Tommy and his family found a place to settle in, they were greeted by a breathtaking scene. The trees lining Section Street were frosted in twinkling white lights, casting a soft glow over the entire town. It was as if the stars themselves had come down from the sky to join in the festivities. The quaint streets of Fairhope, known for their charming shops and cozy restaurants, looked even more enchanting during the holidays. Each storefront was adorned with wreaths, garlands, and twinkling displays that reflected the town's love for Christmas.

The kids were buzzing with excitement, their faces lighting up as they heard the first distant notes of festive music echoing down the street. The parade had begun.

"Look, there's Santa!" Ali pointed out as the jolly figure came into view.

Santa Claus, seated atop a grand float, looked like he had come straight from the North Pole. His warm smile, rosy cheeks, and plump belly were everything a child could hope for in St. Nick. He laughed and danced to "Here Comes Santa Claus" and called out his trademark "Ho! Ho! Ho!"

Noah, however, was far more captivated by what came next. A bright red firetruck, its sirens silent but its frame adorned with colorful, blinking lights, slowly rolled down the street. Firefighters stood on the truck, tossing candy canes and waving to the crowd.

"Dad, look! The firetruck!" Noah's voice was filled with awe.

Tommy couldn't help but smile as he glanced down at his son. Noah dreamt of becoming a firefighter and seeing his eyes light up as the firetruck passed by made all of Tommy's stress from earlier in the day seem insignificant.

"Maybe one day you'll be up there," Tommy said while giving him a pat on the back.

Noah grinned, clutching the candy cane he had just caught from one of the firefighters.

As the parade continued, there were twinkling carriages, festive marching bands, and dancers dressed as elves and snowflakes, moving in perfect rhythm to the Christmas music that filled the air. The whole town seemed to come alive, celebrating the season together.

Ali, standing next to Tommy, smiled softly as she watched the joy on the kids' faces.

The parade continued long into the evening, but to Tommy, it felt like it ended too soon. As the last float passed by and the crowd began to disperse, he wrapped his arm around Ali's shoulders, pulling her close. "Not bad," he said, his voice soft in the crisp night air.

"Not bad at all," Ali agreed, leaning into him as they watched the kids skip ahead, still buzzing with excitement.

CHAPTER 14

Ali

At the office, Ali stared at the calendar on her desk. Ten days until Christmas. She and her colleagues had made it a daily ritual to count down, but each morning the reminder brought her more anxiety than excitement. As much as she loved the holiday season, the looming sense of panic grew with every passing day. There was so much still left to do, and she had no control or knowledge that it will get completed.

Her eyes darted to the circled date on the calendar, just five days until the neighborhood holiday party at their house. She grabbed her phone wondering what Tommy had planned for the party, tempted to ask him but she hesitated and laid her phone back down. Their agreement was clear: Tommy was in charge of the entire event, but despite the arrangement, Ali couldn't shake the feeling that the house needed to be spotless for their guests. No way could she let people in if things were not perfect. I'll focus on cleaning over the next few days, she decided.

It wasn't the role she'd wanted this year, but no matter how hard she tried to let go of the reins, some things felt non-negotiable. And if a few decorations happened to get "adjusted" while she was tidying up, well, that didn't count as breaking their deal... right?

After work, Ali headed to the local shopping district, determined to find the perfect gift for the neighborhood exchange. The exchange had become somewhat of a competitive tradition, and she always liked to make a strong showing. But as she wandered from shop to shop, her attention drifted, distracted by festive displays and holiday sales. She had come with a single purpose in mind, but the temptation to shop for more lingered.

In one boutique, a soft, cream-colored blouse caught her eye. It was perfect for her mother, with intricate stitching that Ali knew she'd love. She smiled, imagining her mom's reaction. A few stores down, a thick, padded stadium seat caught her attention, exactly what her stepfather needed for Pierce's baseball games this spring. He'd get so much use out of this, she thought, picturing him sitting proudly at the games, a grin on his face. For a moment, she considered purchasing both gifts, feeling the familiar pull to cross them off her list.

But then she stopped herself, the weight of her promise to Tommy sinking in. He was handling the gifts this year. Ali sighed, reluctantly putting the items back on the shelves. She had to honor their deal, but it wasn't easy.

Letting go of control wasn't just hard, it was maddening.

Ali forced herself to focus on her gift for the neighborhood exchange. Eventually, she wandered into a local gourmet shop known for its beautifully crafted bottles of balsamic vinegar and olive oil. After perusing the shelves, she settled on a cranberry-infused balsamic vinegar and her personal favorite, a bottle of white truffle oil. Not only were the bottles practically works of art, stunning enough to display on a kitchen counter, but their rich flavors would elevate any holiday meal. These are perfect, she thought with a chuckle, envisioning the other women fighting over her gift.

While she was there, she also picked up a small bag of candied walnuts, thinking they would be a nice treat to have around the house, and a few extra stocking stuffers for Tommy, including a sleek, stainless-steel pocketknife that caught her eye, it would be practical for his outdoor adventures with the kids. She added a small box of gourmet chocolates and a pair of Charlie Brown Christmas socks. With a few other items she already had at home, his stocking would be full.

It wasn't the all-out shopping spree she yearned for, but it scratched the itch just enough. Ali left the store with her arms full and feeling mostly satisfied, although there was a small part of her that wanted to go back for the blouse and stadium seat.

On the drive home, her mind raced through the tasks for the week: clean the house, wrap the gifts, and finalize party plans with Tommy or at least find out what they were. Christmas was coming fast, but at least tonight, she felt a small sense of accomplishment.

After work every day that week, Ali dove headfirst into her mission: deep cleaning the house. She armed herself with an arsenal of cleaning supplies and a fierce determination. Dusting, vacuuming, scrubbing—she attacked every corner with precision, knowing that soon their home would be filled with friends, laughter, and the clinking of glasses.

But as much as Ali tried to focus, the kids were not making things easy. Maddie and Noah's excitement for winter break turned them into tornados of energy.

"Noah, stop jumping on the couch!" Ali called from the kitchen, where she was wiping down the countertops for the third time that day.

Noah, giggling, immediately launched himself off the cushions and landed with a thud. "But it's almost Christmas, Mommy! I can't wait!"

Pierce was not much better, reverting to his childish antics. He was barreling through the house, a Nerf blaster in hand, taking shots at his siblings. "Watch out, Mom! I'm on a mission!" he yelled, narrowly missing her with a foam dart. Ali sighed but couldn't help smiling. At least they're happy and oblivious to my anxiety, she thought.

Despite the chaos, Ali pushed through. By the time the kids were tucked into bed the night before the party, the house sparkled. The floors gleamed, the furniture was polished, and every surface felt fresh and ready for guests. The house felt festive, and she was finally starting to feel more in control of things.

With the house ready, Ali decided to take some time for herself. She poured herself a glass of eggnog, extra creamy with a dash of cinnamon, and cranked up her favorite Christmas playlist. She headed to her bedroom, eggnog in hand, and started trying on outfits for the party. Ali's sense of style was impeccable yet practical, favoring classic, timeless pieces with a modern twist. She gravitated toward structured blazers, tailored jeans, and chic dresses, always accessorized with thoughtful details, whether it was a delicate necklace, a signature watch, or the perfect pair of shoes.

The excitement of hosting their friends, despite all the pressure, was starting to bubble up. Standing in front of her full-length mirror, she twirled in a deep green dress, watching as the fabric shimmered under the soft light. It was elegant and festive, but she wondered if it might be too much.

"Hmm, maybe something more casual?" she said aloud.

She swapped the dress for a pair of high-waisted jeans and a cozy red sweater with silver snowflakes stitched along the sleeves and Tori Burch flats. Looking in the mirror, she grinned. This feels right. Casual, but festive enough for a night of good food, drinks, and laughter with friends.

The music filled the room as she played with different accessories—scarves, boots, and jewelry—each combination adding a different layer to the night's possibilities. The whole process was like a mini celebration for herself. She hadn't felt this light since her crazy karaoke night.

Ali sank onto the edge of her bed, sipping her eggnog and humming along to the music, feeling a warmth spread through her that wasn't just from the drink. The house was clean, the party plans were mostly in place, and things were starting to feel like Christmas again.

CHAPTER 15

Tommy

It was finally the day of the neighborhood holiday party, and the house buzzed with anticipation. Tommy had everything under control, or so he told himself. He was feeling confident, standing over the kitchen counter, preparing the main course: prime rib. He'd made it before, and though it was ambitious, he was sure he could pull it off.

All the kids, even Pierce, who at sixteen still loved spending time with Ali's mom and stepdad, Grammy and Pop, had been scooped up earlier for a sleepover, leaving the house gloriously quiet—the perfect atmosphere for final party preparations. Ali's Christmas playlist currently playing "Let It Snow, Let It Snow, Let It Snow" drifted through the rooms, set at that perfect volume where you could enjoy it but still easily have a conversation.

The champagne Tommy had picked up yesterday was

chilling in the refrigerator, ready to be popped later in the evening. The prime rib was roasting in the oven, filling the house with an aroma that was sure to impress their guests. Everything looked like it was falling into place.

Tommy was in the middle of preparing the specialty drink, The Grinch Cocktail, a festive concoction he found online imagining everyone toasting with the fun, Christmas-themed drink while laughing at the ridiculousness of it all.

Grinch Cocktail

- ☐ 1.5 ounces Midori liqueur
- ☐ 1-ounce clear rum
- ☐ 5 ounces soda water
- ☐ 1 maraschino cherry

As Tommy poured the soda and rum into the shaker, Ali descended the stairs. He looked up and immediately was reminded how lucky he was to be her husband. She looked stunning in a festive yet understated outfit, her smile lighting up the room as much as the twinkle lights on the tree.

"You look amazing," Tommy said, admiring her. For all the stress they'd both been through this holiday season, seeing her like this made him feel grounded again.

"Thanks," Ali replied, as she stepped into the kitchen. She glanced at the cocktail shaker in his hand. "What's that?"

"Ah, this is the Grinch Cocktail," Tommy said, with a bit too much pride in his voice. "I found it online. It's going to be the drink of the night."

Ali scanned the recipe on the counter, her brow raised as she read through the ingredients. "Midori, rum, soda water… interesting combination." She looked at Tommy, who was rummaging through the cabinets.

Tommy reached for the bottle of Midori, his hand hovering over an empty spot. A sudden wave of panic hit him. "No… no, no, no," he muttered, eyes darting around the kitchen.

Ali's curiosity turned to concern. "What's wrong?"

Tommy groaned, rubbing his hands over his face. "I forgot to buy the Midori, I meant to pick it up today. It's what makes the drink green. Without it, it's just… rum and soda water."

Ali smirked. "And you really want people to drink this?"

Tommy gave her a helpless shrug. "It's supposed to be festive! The green is what makes it fun and 'Grinchy.'"

Biting her lip to keep from laughing outright, Ali shook her head. "Tommy, I'm sorry, but that sounds awful. I don't think anyone's going to care if the Grinch drink isn't the right shade of green."

Tommy let out a deep sigh, shoulders slumping. "I should've remembered though. It's… I didn't want to mess up."

Seeing how deflated he looked, Ali softened. She knew how hard he had been trying to take the reins this holiday season. "Hey," she said gently, "it's not a big deal. I'll run out and grab the Midori. Let me help with this one, okay?"

Tommy shook his head, guilt flickering in his eyes. "You don't have to do that. It's my mess-up, not yours. I'll figure it out."

Ali stepped closer, resting her hand on his arm. "You would do it for me. Besides, if it means keeping your festive green punch dreams alive, I'm all for it."

Tommy chuckled softly, the tension easing from his face, "thanks" the weight of the forgotten Midori starting to lift. He leaned across the counter and gave her a little kiss.

As she headed out the door, Tommy took a deep breath. The house was ready, the food was cooking, and now, thanks to Ali, his signature drink wouldn't be a disaster. They were showing up for each other and that, Tommy realized, was the only thing that really mattered.

He went back to his work, adjusting the music slightly and straightening up the already-clean kitchen admiring Ali's hard work making the house shine and noticing with a smirk that she had moved some decorations around, despite their agreement to leave them as they were. He just laughed to himself and shook his head. Feeling a sense of calm, he hadn't felt in days, Tommy knew the holiday party was going to be a success, even if the Grinch Cocktail wasn't as popular as he had hoped.

Ali returned with the Midori in hand, and Tommy's Cocktail was finally complete. To his surprise, Ali even gave it a sip and said, "You know, it's not that bad." That was all the validation he needed.

Rachel and her husband were the first to arrive, followed by Skip and Mary Anne, with a steady flow of neighbors and friends trickling in after. Luis came a bit later, introducing everyone to his new girlfriend, whom Tommy and Ali were also meeting for the first time. By the time the party was in full swing, about two dozen people were mingling through their home, chatting and laughing. The kitchen island was covered with an impressive spread of appetizers and side dishes, and Tommy's prime rib was already getting rave reviews.

Ali, with a glass of rosé in hand, mingled effortlessly, enjoying the festive buzz of the evening. Tommy, on the other hand, continued drinking his Grinch Cocktail, mostly to encourage others to give it a try. To his relief, it was a hit—well, at least among the more adventurous drinkers.

The gift exchange was, as always, the highlight of the night. The energy in the room picked up as people unwrapped gifts, hoping for something desirable or, at the very least, hilarious. Ali's infused olive oil and balsamic vinegar was a hot commodity, stolen three times throughout the game. Tommy's contribution? A $25 gift card to Rotolo's, because after Noah's party, he figured he owed Tony some extra business.

Of course, there were a few gag gifts in the mix. Luis brought a "Jelly of the Month" calendar, which everyone got a good laugh out of. "Wait, it's just pictures of jelly?" Skip asked while hysterically laughing. "No actual jelly?"

Luis shrugged with a mischievous grin. "Art is subjective."

As the last guest filtered out, Tommy and Ali were both exhausted but content. Tommy glanced at the clock as he rolled into bed next to Ali. Midnight. They had made it through another holiday event, for tonight at least, they could rest easy.

CHAPTER 16

Ali

Ali slept in until ten in the morning after the party, which was the latest she had slept in years. She stretched luxuriously in bed before rolling out, feeling refreshed from the fun evening and the unexpected rest. When she went downstairs, Tommy was already putting away the last remnants of the party. Empty glasses, stray napkins, and the usual post-party debris had disappeared.

Tommy looked up as she entered, a smile spreading across his face. "Morning," he said, handing her a steaming cup of coffee.

Ali accepted it gratefully, wrapping her hands around the warm mug. "Thanks." She took a sip, closing her eyes as the caffeine started to wake her up. "You're up early, considering how late we stayed up."

Tommy chuckled, wiping down the counter. "Yeah, well, figured I'd better finish cleaning up before the kids come back, my parents walk in the door, and the mess starts over."

Ali leaned against the kitchen island, watching him with a fond smile. "The party was great, wasn't it?"

"It was." Tommy shook his head, laughing softly. "I'm still proud of my Grinch drink."

Ali laughed with him. "It wasn't that bad, honestly. But I'll admit, it wouldn't have been my first choice."

"And then there's Mary Anne," Tommy said, pointing toward the living room where a pair of high heels sat forgotten near the couch. "She just… left without her shoes. Walked out barefoot like it was no big deal."

Ali snorted, nearly choking on her coffee. "Oh no. I knew she was a little tipsy, but barefoot? I'll have to check on her later."

Tommy grinned. "I think she had exactly as much fun as she needed. Might need a few aspirin today, though."

"And a few gallons of water," Ali added, shaking her head. "And then there was that cranberry dip. Did you see it? It barely got touched."

"Yeah, who brought that?" Tommy asked, his eyebrows raised. "It was like a brick of gelatin."

Ali laughed, setting her mug down. "I have no idea, but we're definitely not keeping the leftovers."

They stood there for a moment, caught in the warmth of the quiet morning after a successful evening. Ali slid her arms around Tommy's waist and rested her head against his chest, sighing contentedly. "You did a great job," she murmured.

Tommy wrapped his arms around her, pressing a kiss to the top of her head. "Thanks, but I couldn't have done it without you. You saved the Grinch Cocktail, after all."

Ali set her coffee down, savoring the peaceful morning, but then noticed Tommy had gone quiet, a familiar furrow forming in his brow.

"What's on your mind?" she asked, giving him a knowing look.

Tommy sighed heavily, leaning against the counter. "Christmas Eve dinner...I saw the extra Turkey in the freezer, which I need to take out today, the one you bought at Thanksgiving—but that's about it so far. I haven't figured out the sides, desserts, or anything else."

Ali raised an eyebrow and smiled. "The prime rib you made last night was great; people couldn't stop talking about it. You're a better cook than you think, Tommy. You've got this."

Tommy's shoulders relaxed slightly, but he still seemed unconvinced.

Tommy set his coffee down and leaned against the counter. "The kids won't be back for a few hours. What are you going to do with yourself?"

Ali glanced toward the clock and then out the window, where the morning sunlight spilled into the kitchen. "Well, your parents are arriving this afternoon, so I need to get the guest room ready. And there's always laundry, I can't let that pile get too comfortable."

Tommy grinned. "Maybe you just relax for a change."

Ali gave him a playful nudge. "Maybe." But, true to form, she was already heading toward the laundry room, unable to sit still for long. Sorting through piles of clothes, she mentally mapped out her next move, mopping the kitchen once the laundry was going. The house hummed with quiet productivity as she moved from task to task. She enjoyed this feeling of accomplishment and was happy to feel a little control again.

CHAPTER 17

Tommy

Tommy heard the rumble of his parents' car as it pulled into the driveway. He stood at the front door, arms crossed, bracing himself for the whirlwind that was Lucille and Thomas Crawford Senior's arrival.

The car door swung open, and out came his mom, Lucille, in a bright red sweater adorned with sparkling Christmas ornaments. Tommy's father opened the back door, grabbing their newest family member, a tiny, wiry-haired Yorkshire terrier he had gifted to his wife last Christmas, fittingly named Cindy Lou Who, or LuLu for short.

"She's got her Christmas sweater on, too," Lucille announced proudly, gesturing towards the wiggling pup for Tommy to see. LuLu's sweater was striped red and white, complete with a tiny green bow. "Isn't she adorable?"

Tommy grinned. "How could I forget? It's been a whole year of LuLu updates."

Lucille wasn't listening. She was already pulling suitcase after suitcase out of the trunk, stacking them precariously on the driveway. "Thomas, grab that bag, will you? And don't forget the one with my hair products."

Tommy raised an eyebrow. "Mom, how long are you planning to stay?"

"Oh, hush, Tommy," she replied with a wave of her hand. "I didn't know what the weather would be like, so I packed for all occasions. Better safe than sorry!"

By the time they shuffled inside, the foyer was overrun with bags, LuLu was sniffing the baseboards, and Tommy's dad had already begun his show for the kids.

"Watch this, Noah," Thomas Sr. said, pretending to pull a quarter from behind his ear. Noah's eyes widened as he clutched the shiny coin. "How do you do that, Grandpa?"

"A magician never reveals his secrets," his father replied with a wink, before wandering toward the bar and pouring himself a neat glass of Buffalo Trace Bourbon.

Lucille set her sights on the living room, placing her hands on her hips as her eyes swept over the decorations. A cascade of tinsel draped across the mantel, mismatched lights blinked on the tree, and lopsided garland added the final, imperfect touch.

"Well," she began, an amused smile tugging at her lips, "This is... interesting."

Tommy braced himself.

"Is this all you? Because I'd say Hobby Lobby better watch out. They've got competition."

He shook his head at his mother and confidently countered, "What can I say? I'm a man of many talents."

Lucille laughed, adjusting a strand of lights on the tree. "I'll give you points for effort. Ali must be hating this."

"She's been having a great time," Tommy muttered.

"I bet she has," Lucille replied, still chuckling as she stepped back to admire the scene. "This whole switch idea is going to be the gift that keeps on giving, at least for me."

"Glad my struggles are so entertaining," he muttered, but his mom just patted his cheek.

"Lighten up, honey. I am going to head upstairs. I need to unpack before dinner."

Tommy helped take her bags upstairs, watching as she inspected every corner of the room. "Ali?" she declared, focusing on the fluffed pillows.

"Yes, Mother, she couldn't let me have all the fun. She got your room ready this morning," he replied, a touch defensively.

"I can tell," she said with a smile.

When he headed back downstairs, the house was alive with chaos. LuLu was trotting after Noah, who had discovered that the little dog loved chasing balls of wrapping paper. Pierce was catching up with his grandfather, giving Thomas Sr. the rundown on his football highlights, reliving his interception during the last game of the season, while Maddie ran behind Noah and snapped a picture of LuLu to send to her friends.

Tommy stood at the edge of it all, a mixture of amusement and exasperation washing over him. His parents were here, and their presence was already filling the house with noise, laughter, and a healthy dose of his mom's opinions. He knew the next few days would be anything but peaceful, but as he watched his dad pull another quarter from behind Noah's ear, Tommy could not help but smile.

This was Christmas with the Crawfords: Loud, chaotic, and completely unforgettable.

CHAPTER 18

Ali

Monday, December 22nd, marked the start of a countdown Ali had been eagerly anticipating. Just two more days of work, then she would be on winter break, a full 10 days when the campus completely shut down for the Christmas and New Year's holidays. The light at the end of the tunnel was so close she could practically feel it. But before her well-earned time off, there was one last work tradition she always looked forward to, the annual holiday lunch. Typically, for Ali, it was one of the rare events she could just attend without having to be in charge or worrying about making sure everything went smoothly. She could relax and enjoy herself.

As she walked into the community college's festively decorated staff lounge, Ali smiled. A small but jolly tree stood in one corner, adorned with red and gold ornaments, and the tables were covered with green plastic tablecloths. The scent of baked ham wafted from the buffet table, making her stomach growl. After filling her plate, she spotted Rachel waving from a table near the window and made her way over, eager to sit down and chat.

Ali slid into the chair beside Rachel and greeted the rest of the table, which was filled with a few other colleagues, including Jess and Claire, who had both worked in admissions at the college for years. Everyone was in good spirits, chatting about their holiday plans.

"So," Rachel began, flashing Ali a mischievous grin and directing the conversation towards the other members of the table as she took a bite of mashed potatoes, "Have you heard about the Christmas swap Ali made with Tommy this year?"

"What swap?" Jess asked, leaning in with interest.

"Ali and Tommy made this deal," Rachel explained, her eyes sparkling with amusement. "He's doing all of her Christmas tasks this year, shopping, cards, everything— and she's doing his, which means Ali has been on the roof putting up lights and she is frying the turkey this year."

The table erupted into laughter. "No way!" Claire said, nearly choking on her soda. "That's genius!"

Ali grinned. "It's been... entertaining, to say the least. Tommy's been a little stressed, but he is pulling it off. And putting the outside lights up was a nightmare. I don't ever want to get on a ladder that high again."

Jess's eyes widened, "I think I could manage the ladder, but there's no way I could fry a turkey. I'd burn the house down."

Ali forced a laugh. "Oh, I've been watching tutorial YouTube videos at night after Tommy goes to bed. It's frightening."

Claire shook her head, "I've been running around like crazy trying to get everything done. The thought of my husband handling all the shopping. Never gonna happen."

"Same," Jess added, stabbing her fork into a piece of ham. "I've still got gifts to wrap, and I'm just skipping Christmas cards at this point."

Ali leaned back in her chair as she tried to hide her real feelings of unease. She responded to their banter, "Well, I actually miss the shopping and frantic planning, but I highly recommend the swap for one year, if you can convince your husbands to agree to it."

Rachel laughed, raising her glass, "To Ali, for setting the bar high."

As their plastic cups touched for a toast, Ali faked a smile. She could not help but feel nervous, not knowing what was planned for the main events, Christmas Eve and Christmas Day. But for now, she was content to sit back, enjoy her lunch, and share a few laughs with her friends.

As lunch continued, Rachel leaned closer, lowering her voice slightly. "How are you holding up with the last-minute news about Tommy's parents?"

Ali smirked, "Oh, you mean the fact that they announced they were coming with about five minutes' notice? I should be furious, but honestly, I can't help but laugh. Tommy's mom is giving him such a hard time about the decorations and the whole switch idea. I almost feel sorry for him."

"Almost," Jess teased, grinning.

"Almost," Ali confirmed with a laugh. "My in-laws are a little overbearing sometimes, but I've got to admit, it's nice to have them here; they're great with the kids. Lucille is hysterical with her little Yorkie, Lulu. That dog prances around in her Christmas sweaters like she owns the place, and the kids love having her around."

"How cute!" Claire said, chuckling.

"Sounds like you're in for a memorable Christmas," Rachel said with a wink.

"Memorable is one word for it," Ali replied, sipping her drink. "Tommy wanted a challenge, and he got one."

The rest of the lunch passed in easy conversation and laughter, but as Ali drove home later that afternoon, she found herself wondering how Tommy was really handling the added chaos.

CHAPTER 19

Tommy

Christmas Eve morning arrived crisp and clear, and Tommy, who was finally off work for the next few days, was ready to embrace the holiday spirit. Everything was covered at the station, and now he needed to make sure everything was covered at home, especially tonight's dinner, which had become his new source of stress.

He woke up with a to-do list swirling in his head: last-minute presents to buy, a grocery store trip for all of the items still missing for dinner, and one big problem was making him panic. Noah's dinosaur, the big gift Tommy ordered, had not arrived. The shipping delay was out of his control, but he needed to figure out a backup plan.

As Tommy stretched and climbed out of bed, the sounds of his family stirring brought a small sense of comfort. The kids were already buzzing with excitement, their chatter about presents and holiday fun filling the house.

Downstairs, the rich aroma of gravy and biscuits wafted through the air. Ali was already in the kitchen preparing breakfast. His mother, ever festive, popped a bottle of champagne, mixing Christmas Eve Poinsettias, a simple mix of cranberry juice, champagne, and a splash of triple sec as she chatted with Ali.

Tommy made his way into the kitchen, kissed Ali on the cheek, and accepted a Poinsettia from his mother. "You two are spoiling us," he said with a grin.

"It's Christmas Eve. Why not?" Ali replied, handing him a plate just as the kids ran into the room, drawn by the irresistible smell of breakfast.

For a little while, everything felt perfect. The house was alive with warmth and laughter, everyone in high spirits as they lingered at the breakfast table. Even Tommy felt the weight on his shoulders lift slightly. But, as always, perfection never lasted long.

As they dug into their meal, the conversation turned toward Tommy's weak spot, Christmas Eve dinner. His mother, her champagne clearly loosening her tongue, leaned in with a curious smile. "So, Tommy," she began, cheerful but pointed, "since you are in charge, what's the plan for the meal tonight?"

"Ali's frying the turkey," he said, trying to sound breezy but feeling a knot tighten in his stomach.

Lucille wasn't satisfied. "And what are we having with the turkey?"

"Stuffing, mashed potatoes, brussel sprouts, dinner rolls and I'm picking up pies today," Tommy snapped back, a little more sharply than he intended. He quickly softened, scrambling to sound composed. "I have it under control."

His mother raised an eyebrow. "Stove Top stuffing?" she asked with a chuckle, her skepticism cutting deep.

"Yes, Stove Top. The kids love it, and it's surprisingly good," he shot back, standing his ground. "And the mashed potatoes will be homemade." The room was silent, so Tommy took this opportunity to change the subject. Pivoting away from his mother's lack of faith, he turned to the kids with a grin. "Alright, let's settle this once and for all—is *Die Hard* a Christmas movie?"

The older kids immediately jumped in, passionately arguing their sides, the debate injecting levity back into the room. For now, it was enough to distract everyone from his growing anxiety about the day ahead.

After breakfast, with the kids occupied and Ali busy tidying up the remnants of breakfast, Tommy slipped out the door, telling her he had last-minute shopping to do. He made a beeline for the nearest toy store, scanning the shelves for anything that could work as a replacement for the dinosaur Noah had his heart set on. As he walked the crowded aisles, the pressure mounted. It had to be something good, something Noah would be excited about.

Finally, something caught his eye. It was not the dinosaur, but it was something that just might work. Tommy grabbed it, feeling a sense of relief wash over him.

With Noah's big gift covered, Tommy still wanted to pick up a few more presents to place under the tree for all his kids. The mall was a madhouse, crowds of frantic shoppers jostling for space, long lines snaking out of every store, and the constant sound of Christmas music battling with stressed-out voices. He had been so laser-focused on finding exactly what the kids had asked for that he had not had a chance to think about surprising them with extras. Ali always made sure there was a small pile of presents for each child, their Santa requests, plus a few unexpected gifts that lit up their faces on Christmas morning. He wanted to keep that tradition alive, so battling the commotion was worth it.

Later that day, after completing the shopping and a quick trip to the grocery store for the final dinner supplies, the reality started to sink in that everyone was expecting a gourmet meal that night. Tommy still needed to start cooking, and somehow, the list felt longer than ever.

"Do you have everything for dinner?" Ali asked, breaking into his thoughts as she started putting away the clean dishes from the dishwasher.

Tommy rubbed the back of his neck. "Yes, all covered," was what he said, but not what he felt. "Are you ready to fry the turkey?" he countered to Ali.

"All covered." Ali shot back; she mirrored his short response.

By early evening, the family gathered in the living room, the holiday atmosphere starting to fray around the edges. Tommy was knee-deep in kitchen chaos—pots simmering, ingredients scattered, and a timer blaring every few minutes while Ali stood outside with a pot of oil, scrolling frantically on her phone. It was painfully clear that neither of them was ready for dinner, let alone dressed for the Christmas Eve church service.

The kids, already antsy, groaned about having to dress up and go to church, added to the stress. Sensing the tension, Tommy's parents stepped in with a solution. "Why don't we take the kids to church?" Lucille offered, a knowing smile softening her tone. "You two can stay back and finish getting dinner together."

Ali hesitated, but the relief on Tommy's face made the decision easy. "That might actually save us," she admitted, giving her mother-in-law a small smile.

"Great! Kids, grab your coats," Lucille said, ushering them towards the door. "We'll bring them back just in time to eat."

Once the house was quiet, Tommy and Ali exchanged a look, part grateful for the extra time and part saddened to miss the beautiful candlelight service. The sudden silence felt almost eerie. Ali took a deep breath and pulled her hair into a messy bun. "Alright. Let's do this."

The potatoes were boiling, steam rising from the stove as Tommy frantically checked the timer on the rolls, two minutes left. The stuffing was done but keeping it warm without letting the bottom of the pot burn felt like a losing battle. Ali would not have cooked the stuffing or the rolls until the mashed potatoes were finished, what was he thinking? He already felt like he was messing up the entire meal; his timing was completely off.

"Did you salt the potatoes?" Ali called from across the kitchen.

"Uh…" Tommy stared at the pot. "I think so?" He sighed, grabbed the salt, and tossed in a heavy pinch for good measure. "Let's not take any chances." The oven timer beeped, and Tommy pulled the rolls out too fast; one slid off the baking sheet and hit the floor. He stared at it for a second, then groaned as he bent down, grabbed it, and tossed it in the garbage. His first casualty and probably not his last. Tommy wiped his hands on a dish towel, and then he heard a deafening BOOM that rattled the windows.

"What the—" he started, spinning toward the back door.

Ali burst inside, wild-eyed, and frantic, her face smeared with grease and soot. "The turkey exploded!" she yelled.

"What?" Tommy bolted toward the window, his panic rising as thick smoke rolled across the backyard.

"It's on fire!" Ali shrieked, fumbling for her phone. "911? We need the fire department—right now!"

Tommy yanked open the back door to see flames roaring from the turkey fryer, their glow lighting up the yard like an inferno. "Did you read the instructions?" he barked, the words flying out before he could stop them.

"Oh, don't you dare!" Ali pointed at Tommy accusingly.

"Ma'am, is everyone safe?" the 911 operator's voice cut through their shouting, calm and professional amidst the chaos.

"Yes," Ali huffed into the phone, "But we need help now!"

Tommy grabbed the fire extinguisher from the pantry and fumbled with the pin, his hands trembling. "How does this stupid thing work?"

"Oh, for crying out loud," Ali snapped, snatching it from him. She yanked the pin free and stomped toward the flames. "I've got this!"

"Like you had the turkey?" Tommy muttered under his breath but loud enough for her to hear.

The glare she threw back at him could have extinguished the fire faster than foam.

The fire in the fryer blazed on as Ali wrestled with the extinguisher, the flames mocking her efforts. Suddenly, the sound of sirens cut through the evening air.

"Perfect," Tommy muttered, his shoulders slumping. "The whole neighborhood's about to see this circus."

The red lights of the fire truck flickered through the smoke as it screeched to a halt in the driveway. Firefighters poured out, their boots hitting the ground quickly.

"Back away from the fryer!" one of them barked, motioning for them to step aside.

Ali handed off the extinguisher with a sheepish look, "It's just the fryer, we're fine. Really."

But as the firefighters worked to douse the flames, a familiar high-pitched BEEP, BEEP, BEEP erupted from the house.

"Oh no," Ali groaned, clutching her soot-streaked forehead.

"The potatoes! I had them on the highest temperature to speed up the boiling," Tommy gasped, bolting toward the kitchen.

He stumbled into a light haze of smoke that was quickly getting heavier. "Dammit!" he yelled into the empty room, he grabbed a dish towel and frantically fanned the blaring smoke detector overhead. On the stove, the pot of potatoes boiled over violently. Thick, starchy water had overflowed the rim and spilled down the sides, hissing as it hit the open gas flame below. The water sizzled on contact, creating steam and a smoky film that quickly rose and filled the kitchen. The combination of steam and smoke had crept upward and tripped the fire alarm.

He spun toward the pot, steam continued to rise, as water ran across the burner grates and down into the metal catch pans, leaving behind a sticky, white residue. In his rush, he reached for the handle without a towel and yelped, immediately dropping the scalding pot onto the counter with a loud clang. His palm throbbed, but he barely noticed, as his blood pressure spiked while he surveyed the chaos: a scorched burner, steam filling the room, and the shrill alarm still wailing overhead.

Ali stormed into the disastrous scene; "What now?" she shouted, slamming her hands onto the counter.

Tommy glared at his wife. "Oh, so now it's my fault?"

"Yes! All this is your fault!" Ali snapped. "Switching Christmas was your idea!"

"I remember, sweetheart," he bit back. He saw her eyes narrow; she hated it when he called her that, and he knew it.

"Where's the dog?" he barked, coughing through the haze.

"We don't have a dog!" Ali snapped back before remembering, "LuLu!" Ali shouted, squinting through the chaos. A small blur of fur darted past her legs, yipping madly as if to say, *You're on your own.* "Under the couch!" Ali yelled, dropping to her knees. She reached under the furniture, trying to coax the tiny dog out. "Lulu, come here!" Ali pleaded, but the Yorkie barked defiantly.

Just then, the firefighters burst into the kitchen, their boots thudding against the hardwood floor. One stopped when he noticed the smokey kitchen. "What's burning now?"

Ali gestured helplessly toward the stove. "The potatoes boiled over scorching the stovetop and I'm pretty sure the stuffing is burnt too."

The firefighter arched a brow and tried to lighten the mood as he glared into the pots, "This may be the first time I've seen someone ruin Stovetop Stuffing," he said gesturing towards the box on the counter as he laughed.

The chaos seemed to hit its peak as the smoke alarm continued its ear-piercing shriek and the dog continued to bark. Then one of the firefighters called out, "I smell burnt rubber."

They all bolted back outside, where another firefighter was already extinguishing the garden hose that had somehow melted against the still-smoking turkey fryer.

Ali's eyes widened, "The hose!"

Tommy looked at Ali, who was about to cry, and pulled her in for a hug. Both were covered in soot and sweat, surrounded by a ruined meal, a melted hose, and a smug-looking Yorkie who finally left her safe spot under the couch to join the excitement in the backyard.

The front door burst open while the firefighters rolled up their hoses and packed away their equipment. "We saw the firetrucks! What happened?" Lucille's voice rang out, laced with concern, and she waved the smoky smell away from her nose. The kids barreled into the house behind her, wide-eyed and frantic.

"Is everything okay?" Maddie cried, running to her mother.

"Why are there firemen here?" Pierce demanded, already scanning the room for evidence of catastrophe.

"Firefighters, cool!" Noah exclaimed. "Did the house burn down?" He looked around, clearly seeing it still standing, despite the smoke in the air.

Tommy and Ali, covered in ash, turned from where they were huddled near the stove, both looking frazzled.

"It's fine, kids. Everything's fine," Tommy said, holding up his hands in what he hoped was a calming gesture.

"Doesn't look fine," Tommy's father, said pointedly, eyeing the smoke still faintly lingering in the room.

LuLu chose that moment to bark wildly at a firefighter passing through the kitchen to grab a Halligan tool that had been left behind.

"Lulu!" Lucille gushed, lunging for the Yorkie and scooping her up protectively.

"So, what happened?" Pierce asked, his tone a mix of sarcasm and amazement.

"It was the turkey," Ali admitted sheepishly.

"The turkey exploded," Tommy added dramatically.

"Exploded?" Maddie questioned.

Thomas Sr., Lucille, Pierce, Maddie, and Noah stood frozen at the kitchen window, eyes wide, staring at the horrific scene outside.

The backyard looked like a war zone. The once-green grass was scorched black in a wide, uneven circle. The metal pot, now warped and half-melted, lay crooked on its side, smoke still curling from beneath it. Ash clung to the rose bush nearby, its leaves drowned from the strong spray of the fire hose. The air was thick with the sharp scent of burnt meat and something metallic.

Ali, trembling, spoke. Her voice was shaky, barely above a whisper. "I had just walked away to get my phone from the back porch. I could've been standing right there…" She stared at the charred ground, her breath catching at the realization that she could have been badly hurt.

Lucille gently placed a hand on her shoulder, her own face pale. "You were lucky," she said quietly, glancing at Tommy, who stood with a solemn expression. "You both were."

Even the kids, usually quick to ask questions or make jokes, said nothing. They just stood there, eyes fixed on the backyard, as the reality of the evening's events settled in.

One of the firefighters approached, which broke the tension. He tipped his helmet politely toward the family, "Everything's under control now. No lasting damage, just a little excitement. You've got quite the story for the Christmas books."

"Well, that's one way to put it," Lucille replied, looking between Tommy and Ali like they were defiant teenagers.

As the firefighter turned to leave, a small voice piped up. "Excuse me, sir?"

The firefighter, a burly man with a kind smile, crouched slightly to meet Noah's gaze. "What's up, little man?"

Noah tugged nervously at his sweater and said, "I—I wanna be a firefighter when I grow up. Did you really put out a turkey fire?"

The firefighter chuckled, glancing with the family at the charred remains of the fryer safely outside. "Sure did. But don't worry, everything is okay now. You know, most fires we get called to during the holidays are because of things like this."

Noah's eyes widened. "Really? You fight turkey fires a lot?"

"Not just turkeys," the firefighter replied with a wink. "We've seen all kinds of stuff. Christmas trees, candles, heaters. You have got to be really careful during the holidays."

Noah nodded thoughtfully, as if absorbing a crucial life lesson. "I'll remember that when I'm a firefighter."

The man smiled and patted Noah's shoulder. "Good man. We're always looking for brave recruits like you. If you ever want to come visit the fire station, you tell your parents, and we'll give you the grand tour."

Noah's face lit up like the Christmas tree in the living room. "Really? Can I go to the fire station, Dad?"

Tommy, leaning against the counter with a slightly dazed expression, managed a smile. "Sure thing, buddy, but not tonight."

"That smell is definitely not going to be dinner," Pierce said with a smirk, eyeing the charred remains of the meal, as the last firefighter walked out the front door.

"Nope, it's gone," Tommy muttered, his voice flat with frustration.

Lucille chimed in, stepping in with her usual efficiency. "Just in case tonight's dinner was a bust, I made reservations at The Grand Hotel in Point Clear. We'll have a good holiday meal there."

Tommy shot a glance at his mother, his sarcasm spilling forth. "Thanks for the vote of confidence, Mom." He could feel the weight of his failure and her silent judgment.

Ali, sensing Tommy's frustration, stepped in to defend him. "This is on me. I was supposed to have the turkey under control, but... well, we can all see how that turned out." She looked at Tommy, giving him a reassuring nod.

Tommy let out a deep sigh, the tension in his chest easing just slightly. His pride was still bruised, but it was

Christmas Eve, "Alright, fine. Let's go. We'll have dinner at The Grand."

With the decision made, Thomas Senior, Lucille, and the kids cleaned the kitchen while Tommy and Ali showered for dinner.

CHAPTER 20

Ali

An hour later, the family piled into the car and headed for The Grand Hotel in Point Clear, where Tommy's mother had saved the evening with her dinner reservation at the famous resort, known for its over-the-top holiday decorations and traditions.

As they entered the gates of the hotel, the atmosphere was nothing short of magical. The Grand Holiday Stroll was in full swing, with adorned lampposts lighting the way, and Santa's Workshop nestled within the southern foliage. Tommy caught a glimpse of an elf by the lagoon, a whimsical sight that actually brought a smile to his face.

The walk toward the main building was mesmerizing. Gleaming arches lit the brick pathway around the lagoon, and the towering, sparkling bow on the front of the historic main building peeked above the treetops. As they walked, they passed by the three fountains, which glittered in the soft glow of holiday lights. The "Bent Oak," a hundred-year-old tree donned with gigantic, illuminated ornaments, provided the perfect backdrop for a family photo.

"Come on, just one picture," Ali coaxed as Noah fidgeted. Pierce, stepping into his big brother role, struck a goofy pose to encourage his siblings to join in.

Once the photos were snapped, the family continued to soak in the decorations. The Grand Live Oak stood as the centerpiece, draped in over 23,700 twinkling holiday lights. The whole scene was magical, and even Tommy had to admit it was pretty cool. The inside of the resort was just as breathtaking. The Grand Hall bustled with carolers, and the Gingerbread Display in the lobby was as grand as ever. Everywhere they turned, the scent of Christmas and gourmet hot beverages filled the air. The family made their way to dinner, greeted by the warm, festive atmosphere of The Grand's famous Christmas Eve feast.

The meal was undeniably elegant, a festive spread that seemed fit for a magazine cover. The evening began with a crisp salad of mixed greens, cranberries, and goat cheese, drizzled with a tangy vinaigrette. At the carving station, succulent roast beef and honey-glazed ham were served alongside creamy potatoes au gratin and perfectly seasoned green bean almondine. Warm, homemade dinner rolls with honey butter melted in their mouths, and the meal ended with decadent chocolate lava cakes, topped with cherries for a holiday flourish. It was divine, everything a Christmas dinner should be; however, Ali and Tommy could not help glance at each other with a shared understanding that they both would rather be at home.

Ali took a deep breath, reminding herself that the holidays were about family and togetherness, even if things did not go exactly as planned. She just needed to keep that in mind as the night went on, pushing the turkey crisis to the back of her thoughts.

A few hours later, they pulled into the driveway, full and ready for bed, but Ali's heart sank at the sight of their dark house. Not a single twinkle of Christmas lights. The rest of the neighborhood glowed with holiday cheer, but their home stood out, dark and lifeless.

"Why are the lights off?" Maddie asked from the backseat, her voice cutting through the car's quiet hum.

Tommy glanced at Ali, and the tension she had been feeling during the day only thickened. This was on her, again. She had been in charge of the lights this year, and clearly, something had gone very wrong.

"We probably blew a fuse," Ali said, trying to keep calm. "I'll fix it."

"But how will Santa see our house if the lights aren't on?" Noah asked, his voice filled with concern, "what if he skips us?"

Ali swallowed a sigh. The last thing she needed was to add "Santa's navigation" to her list of Christmas troubles. "Don't worry, guys," she said, trying to sound reassuring. "I'll have the lights back on in no time."

Tommy's father, who had been observing the disasters unfold, shook his head. "This is what happens when you switch things up. The Christmas switch was a terrible idea."

Ali glanced at Tommy, who looked as though he might respond, but instead, he offered to get the kids inside and into pajamas, and for that, she was grateful. "All right, everybody out. Flashlight party," Tommy said, pulling out his phone and turning on the flashlight app. Pierce played along, also pulling out his phone and turning on the flashlight, Noah giggled, while Maddie rolled her eyes, too cool to be impressed by such antics.

Ali stayed outside for a moment longer, staring up at the house. Her stomach knotted. She knew she had to handle this; how hard could it be to fix?

Inside, Tommy guided the rest of the family upstairs, navigating the hallways in the dark with ease, by the light of his phone. Meanwhile, Ali opened the fuse box in the garage and tried to make sense of it. She flicked a few switches but was met with nothing but more darkness.

She felt the weight of it all, the Christmas switch, the undone tasks, the ruined meal, and now this. She had wanted everything to go smoothly. But here she was, in the cold garage, feeling completely out of her depth.

Tommy called out from the hallway, "Kids are settled. Need help?"

"No, I've got it!" Ali lied, fumbling through the switches again, refusing to admit defeat.

After three more failed attempts, she stood there in the garage, staring at the confusing panel of switches. A deep sigh escaped her, the cold of the garage making her shiver. She rubbed her arms and stared at the mess of fuses.

Finally, she trudged back inside, her pride deflated. Tommy was waiting in the kitchen staring at his phone which was casting a dim glow on his face.

"Alright," she said quietly, feeling outsmarted by the fuse box and knowing she had admitted defeat. "I need help. I have no idea what I'm doing out there."

Tommy smiled softly, not teasing or rubbing it in. "Let's get those lights back on," he said as he grabbed the flashlight from under the kitchen sink.

She followed him into the garage, watching as he effortlessly flicked a few switches in the fuse box, clearly more confident than she had felt. Within moments, the lights inside the house flickered back to life, followed by the Christmas lights outside, bursting into a colorful glow.

Ali sighed, relief washing over her. "I got them ready for you," she joked, trying to lighten her embarrassment.

Tommy chuckled, giving her a gentle hug as they stood there for a moment seeing the warmth of the outside Christmas lights through the garage window.

However, their holiday spirit was short-lived. Back inside, Tommy walked into the kitchen with his arms full of red, green, and silver sparkling wrapping paper, bows, and bags. "I've still got a lot of wrapping to do," he said, almost cheerfully.

Ali sighed, her hands rubbing her temples as she felt her chest tighten with anxiety, noticing the pile of unwrapped gifts that still needed to be tackled. Her voice was tight as she asked, "You haven't started wrapping?"

Tommy grimaced. "I… didn't get to it yet. We've been a little busy."

For a moment, she felt the urge to explode in frustration at ending up in another mess. She started to speak but then closed her mouth and let out a long exhale, reminding herself that getting angry would not solve anything, plus she owed him one for the lights.

After a few beats, she shook her head, gathering her composure. "Okay," she said finally. "Wrapping takes me hours, if we do it together, it will go quicker."

Tommy gave her a grateful, sheepish look, "I'm in."

Ali handed Tommy a roll of wrapping paper. "We'd better hurry, or we'll still be wrapping when the kids wake up."

Tommy chuckled, rolling his eyes as he started cutting paper for the first gift. "I'll do my best."

Ali looking at the stack of gifts asked, "Hey… where is Noah's dinosaur? The one he has been asking for. I don't see it here."

Tommy's face immediately fell. He shifted awkwardly, avoiding her gaze. "Uh, no. It didn't get shipped in time. I meant to tell you, but we've been a little distracted." He could see the distress on her face and lifted his hands in mock surrender. "I picked something else that I think he'll love more."

She narrowed her eyes, skeptical. "What did you get?"

Tommy hesitated, clearly wanting to keep the mystery. "You'll see."

Ali groaned, rubbing her forehead again. "Fine. But if he's disappointed…"

"I promise, he won't be," Tommy reassured her.

Ali shook her head, mentally moving on to the next crisis. "Okay, but what about the stockings?"

Tommy froze again, clearly caught off guard. "Uh…"

"You forgot stocking stuffers, didn't you?"

Tommy winced. "Maybe?"

Ali sighed, shaking her head. "Good thing I shopped a little before we made this deal. I have a few things stashed away. I also have some fun snacks and treats hidden from Halloween. Hopefully, Noah won't notice." They spent the next thirty minutes digging through Ali's backup stash of gifts and raiding the pantry for anything that could pass as stocking stuffers.

By the time they collapsed on the couch, surrounded by wrapped presents, it was well past two in the morning. Ali leaned her head back against the cushions, looking at Tommy with tired eyes. "We did it."

"Yeah," Tommy said, yawning. "Barely."

The house was quiet, the kids sound asleep upstairs, unaware of the near disasters their parents had just avoided. In a few hours, it would be Christmas, and despite the chaos, they were as ready as they could be.

Tommy glanced at the clock. "We've got about four hours until the kids wake up."

Ali groaned, closing her eyes. "We need sleep."

"Agreed," Tommy said, pulling a blanket over them both, too exhausted to leave the couch, "Merry Christmas."

"Merry Christmas," Ali mumbled, already half-asleep.

And with that, they drifted off, hoping that when they woke up, they could pull off Christmas morning better than Christmas Eve.

CHAPTER 21

Christmas Day

The Crawford kids came downstairs to find their parents asleep on the couch, which was unusual, but they were too excited to care. The plump Christmas tree, with its twinkling lights and family ornaments, stood proud, surrounded by a sea of brightly wrapped presents. Pierce, Maddie, and Noah's eyes widened with anticipation, their excitement bubbling over.

"Mom, Dad! Wake up!" Maddie squealed, snuggling onto the couch beside them.

Noah wasn't far behind, throwing himself on top of Tommy, while Pierce opted for shaking Ali's shoulder. Tommy and Ali rubbed their eyes, stretched, and slowly sat up, groaning from the late night. They exchanged a sleepy glance, sharing a silent understanding that it was time to wake up.

Ali cracked a smile. "No presents until coffee," she declared, causing the kids to let out a collective groan.

Tommy chuckled. "Rules are rules," he said, heading to the kitchen to start the pot.

Just then, the sound of footsteps approached. Tommy's parents entered the room. "Did someone say coffee?" Tommy's dad teased.

The kids wasted no time kneeling in front of the tree, their eyes glued to the presents, their patience wearing thin. Tommy's mom settled into a chair with a warm smile, watching the anticipation build.

Ali and Tommy returned, mugs in hand, still looking a little rough, but the smell of fresh coffee was enough to revive them. They sat on the floor next to the kids, leaning against the couch. "Alright, let's do this," Tommy said, nodding to Pierce to get things rolling.

Ali pulled out her phone for pictures as Pierce handed out presents, starting with Maddie, who squealed with excitement when she tore open the box to reveal her new skincare products, just what she had been asking for; "she'll have a clean face before breakfast," Pierce joked.

Maddie's other gifts were perfect as well; her two favorites were a gold necklace with an "M" and a pair of AirPods. Tommy smiled, proud of himself.

Pierce was thrilled with the new football in blue and gold, his school colors. He tossed it in the air a few times before moving on to a Fairhope High School hoodie sporting the pirate mascot and a pair of basketball sneakers that Ali had purchased before the switch. Gift cards and cash rounded out his haul, and he could not wait to do some shopping of his own.

Meanwhile, Noah was quietly unwrapping his gifts, but with each one, his face revealed a hint of disappointment. His Lego set and action figures were cool, but they were not what he had been hoping for. He had been asking for one thing: a remote-control dinosaur.

Finally, there was just one present left for him. Everyone's attention turned toward Noah as he began unwrapping the large box. Ali's heart pounded as she watched him slowly peel back the paper. Her breath caught when she caught a glimpse of the words "remote control."

Maybe Tommy pulled it off, she thought.

But as Noah tore off the last bit of wrapping paper, the image of a remote-control firetruck emerged. For a second, there was a pause, but then Noah's eyes lit up. "A firetruck! This is the best gift ever!" he shouted, completely thrilled with the unexpected surprise.

Ali and Tommy exchanged a relieved glance. Noah had wanted to be a firefighter for as long as they could remember, and while it was not the dinosaur he had been hoping for, his genuine happiness over the firetruck was exciting for the whole family.

Tommy let out a breath he didn't know he was holding, feeling a wave of relief wash over him. "I told you he'd love it," he whispered to Ali, who shot him a warm smile.

"You're lucky," she muttered, coming in for a hug.

As the kids dug into their stockings, Ali took a deep sip of her coffee and slipped into the kitchen to preheat the oven for breakfast; she did not need to see the unveiling of the crazy stocking stuffers. Sure, the morning had not gone perfectly; there were some missteps with the presents, but in that moment, with her family around her, the joy in her kids' laughter, and the sparkle of Christmas lights glowing softly from the tree, it all felt right.

As Ali re-entered the family room, she laughed, hearing Pierce yell, "A backscratcher, cool!"

Christmas, after all, was about being together, and no amount of planning or perfect gifts could top that.

After Santa's presents were opened, the smell of cinnamon rolls baking in the oven filled the air, adding to the warmth of the morning. Ali stood in the kitchen, gathering her thoughts, and prepping for the day ahead. "I'll cook the bacon and set out some fruit," she offered, glancing over at Tommy, who was sitting at the table sipping his coffee, momentarily relaxed.

The kids were content, scattered across the house, each playing with their new treasures. Pierce and Thomas Senior threw the football in the backyard, avoiding the turkey mess that still needed to be addressed. Maddie had already retreated to her room to try out her new products, and Noah had his firetruck zooming around the house, sirens blaring as it went, sounding a little too familiar, a little too soon.

It was a wonderful moment, the kind of happiness they wanted to let soak in and lock into their memories. Ali and Tommy both knew it would not last long. By lunchtime, Ali's family would start arriving, and the commotion of Christmas Day would be in full force. Ali's parents, known for their boundless energy, were bringing appetizers, a tradition they had upheld for years. Her sister was responsible for bringing the wine, along with her quirky husband, who always had dad jokes ready to share, and two active kids, providing Maddie and Noah with playmates. Everything was covered.

Ali flipped the bacon in the skillet, watching it sizzle, and then checked on the cinnamon rolls through the oven door. "We've got this," she said more to herself than to Tommy, who grabbed his wife, and kissed her lips while putting his finger in the cinnamon roll icing when she was not looking, so he could steal a quick taste.

"Yeah," Tommy replied, "we do."

Before Ali could respond to the icing stunt, the doorbell rang. Tommy wiped his sticky fingers on a dish towel. "I've got it," he said, heading to the door.

When he opened it, Mary Anne stood there, grinning, and holding a pie with both hands. "Merry Christmas! I had an extra chocolate pecan pie, so I thought I'd bring it over—just in case," she said with a wink.

Tommy laughed as he accepted the pie. "Thanks, Mary Anne. You can never have too many desserts."

Still chuckling, he carried the pie into the kitchen and held it up for Ali to see, "Mary Anne dropped this off."

Ali smirked and set her second cup of coffee down. "She saw the firetrucks. I had to tell her about the dinner disaster."

"Ah, that explains it," Tommy said, shaking his head with a grin. He placed the pie on the counter next to the cherry one he had picked up from Luis's cousin, his lifesaver when he needed cookies for Noah's party. The cherry pie, at least, had survived yesterday's dinner fiasco unscathed.

At noon, the doorbell rang again. Ali's parents arrived first, bringing with them an array of gourmet appetizers that could have rivaled anything Ali might have made herself. There were prosciutto-wrapped figs, stuffed mushrooms, and a charcuterie board piled with assorted cheeses, peppered salami, olives, red grapes, almonds, and sea salt crackers. Her sister was not far behind, armed with an assortment of Chardonnay, Pinot Noir, and Rosé to keep the festivities flowing.

Ali, now comfortably nestled into the lively atmosphere, clinked glasses with her sister, feeling the holiday joy all around. Just as everyone was settling in, Maddie, Noah, and their cousins could no longer contain their excitement. They started buzzing around the tree, eager to exchange presents. The adults glanced at each other, and after a brief debate, they agreed to let the present opening commence.

The kids squealed with excitement as Tommy handed out the gifts. Ali watched nervously, curious to see what he had picked out. Her mother was first, unwrapping a set of Mud Pie stoneware mixing bowls, not the beautiful blouse Ali almost bought, but still a thoughtful choice. Ali's sister and her husband burst into laughter when they opened their gift card to Rotolo's; they had already heard the story from Noah's party. "Perfect," her sister chuckled, shaking her head at her brother-in-law.

"It's my go-to gift this year; everyone loves pizza." Tommy laughed, "The kids' teachers, neighbors, even our mailman will all be visiting Rotolo's in the near future."

Even Ali chuckled at her husband and the efficient way he completed his shopping; purchasing the same gift for everyone had its advantages.

Thomas Sr. grinned widely when he pulled out a brand-new fishing pole. "Nice one, Tommy!" he said, clearly impressed, while Ali's stepdad unwrapped a Fairhope High School sweatshirt matching the same one Pierce opened earlier in the morning, perfect for Pierce's games. Ali felt a surge of pride for her husband's thoughtful choices.

Lucille laughed hysterically as she pulled out two boxes of stovetop stuffing and a new Gordon Ramsay cookbook, holding them up for the family to see. "Oh, this is funny!" she said with a wink, clearly amused by the playful gift.

Ali held her breath as she opened her present. Inside was a pair of simple gold hoop earrings, just right for everyday wear. "I love these," she said softly, smiling at Tommy. She handed him a small, wrapped box, the ornament she had purchased with Rachel. Tommy unwrapped it and laughed, reading aloud, "Family, a little bit of crazy and a whole lot of love. Sounds pretty accurate."

Meanwhile, the kids tore into their presents like little tornadoes. Maddie shrieked in delight over her manicure set, while Noah beamed at the dinosaur action figure from Ali's sister, even though it was not the fancy one he had originally asked for, while Pierce grinned from ear to ear as he counted the money he added to his bulging wallet.

With the gifts exchanged, they all gathered around for a toast. Tommy raised his glass of wine, clearing his throat. "Well, we made it," he began, grinning at the family. "Survived the season of the switch and somehow pulled this off."

Laughter erupted around the table. Even Lucille, who had given him such a challenging time since her arrival, smiled warmly at him.

"Seriously," Tommy continued, "I could not have done this without all of you, and especially without Ali. So, what do you think, sweetheart—switching again next year?"

Before Ali could respond, the house was suddenly plunged into darkness as all the lights went out again. The entire family groaned, but Ali just smirked, stood up, and grabbed the flashlight from the counter.

"No, definitely not, but I've got the lights one more time," she said with a wink at Tommy. This time, though, it did not feel like a disaster. She felt pleased with herself as she flipped the correct switches, confident she could fix this hiccup on her own.

CHAPTER 22

Christmas Night

Ali and Tommy stood silently by Noah's bed, the glow of his nightlight casting soft shadows across the room. He looked so peaceful, his favorite bear clutched tightly in his arms, the covers pulled snugly to his chin.

Tommy leaned down first, brushing a kiss against Noah's forehead. "Goodnight, buddy," he whispered.

Ali followed, smoothing a hand over her son's soft curls. "Sweet dreams, baby."

Noah's sleepy eyes blinked open for a moment. "Best Christmas ever," he murmured, a small, satisfied smile on his lips. Ali's heart swelled, and she glanced up at Tommy, whose grin mirrored her own.

They stepped out of the room, leaving the door slightly ajar, and tiptoed down the hall toward the living room. The house was quiet now, the aftermath of a long, joyful day. They sank onto the couch together, Ali curling her legs underneath her as Tommy stretched his arm across the back of the cushions.

"Did you hear that?" Ali asked, her voice soft. "He said it was the best Christmas ever."

Tommy chuckled, "Not bad for a month where everything was upside down, huh?"

Ali leaned her head against his shoulder, a contented sigh escaping her lips. "I was worried about switching roles this year, just how everything would turn out if I were not in charge of every little detail. But looking back… I don't think I've ever had a Christmas like this."

Tommy tilted his head toward her. "What do you mean?"

She smiled, gazing into the lights on the Christmas tree. "I had time, quality time with Maddie while we worked on the lights, just the two of us. Time to take Pierce to the Christmas market and actually be there with him, instead of worrying about my own shopping. Movie nights with the kids, laughing on the couch together. And then the Christmas parade, it was just relaxing, watching it go by without stressing about what I needed to do next."

She paused, the warmth of the memories filling her. "Even an impromptu night out with the girls. Don't get me wrong, my anxiety was through the roof, but I don't think I've ever had the chance to enjoy Christmas like I did this year."

Tommy nodded, a small smile tugging at his lips. "It's nice to see you… happy."

Ali tilted her head up to look at him, her eyes shining. "I needed this break. As hard as it was to let go, it made me realize what I had been missing. All of the little moments that matter."

Tommy grinned, "Since we started the switch, I've asked myself at least once a day how you do this every year. You're incredible."

Ali blushed, "Minus the exploding turkey, I guess the switch wasn't such a disaster after all."

"Not a disaster at all," Tommy laughed.

They sat together, soaking in the quiet magic of the night, knowing that this Christmas, as different as it was, had been exactly right.

One Year Later

Ali, exhausted but happy, crawled into bed on Christmas Eve and pulled the covers up to her chin with a satisfied sigh. December had once again tried to get the best of her, but this year, she had not just survived; she *had fun*. Real fun.

Their annual trip to Southern Hollow had kicked off the season, but instead of agonizing over height and symmetry, they let Noah pick the tree again, declaring it a new tradition. He selected the crooked one with the big gap on one side, announcing that it was "*the perfect space to display the dinosaur ornament.*" It was. They decorated it together with their collection of sentimental family ornaments, plus red and green embellishments. Some things never change, including Ali's eye for decorating, but this year it felt like a collaboration, not a battle between Pinterest and real life.

Ali volunteered for the radio station's canned food drive with Tommy. There was no spreadsheet, no clipboard, just Christmas music and the warmth of giving back.

At Noah's school Christmas party, she wisely joined forces with two other moms, and Ali felt a sense of relief as they divided and conquered. Tommy showed up, too, but steered clear of the glitter glue station for the ornament craft project.

Girls' Night Out made a triumphant return, with matching pajamas and off-key karaoke. No one had to convince her this year; it was planned a month in advance, on the calendar, in pen.

Tommy resumed outside light duty with Maddie as his assistant, both bundled up on the roof, arguing about which strand was out of sync. He pretended to be annoyed, but Ali knew he loved that time with their daughter.

They split the work for the neighborhood holiday party, Tommy's now-famous prime rib made a repeat appearance, while Ali reclaimed the cocktail bar, whipping up a festive cranberry-pomegranate spritz. She did *not* make Grinch Punch.

Ali joined her family to visit Santa at the mall. They waited in line together, devouring hot chocolate loaded with whipped cream and crushed candy cane sprinkles, and ended the trip with oversized food court pizza slices that dripped grease and enjoyment in equal measure. Ali had more fun than she expected, which had become a theme.

At the Christmas market, she allowed herself to *buy* instead of just browsing like last year, selecting homemade preserves, scented candles, and the world's coziest scarf. She met Pierce by the food trucks, and they shared lunch, just the two of them, laughing at how many napkins he needed for his messy loaded fries.

With Ali back in charge of gift shopping, everything was purchased, wrapped, and stashed away by December 20th. No last-minute panic, no scouring shelves on Christmas Eve.

And perhaps the most shocking change of all, Christmas Eve dinner? They returned to The Grand Hotel. No turkey explosions. No kitchen disasters. Just linen napkins, warm rolls, and zero stress. The whole family agreed: frying a turkey was officially *retired*.

As she lay there, in the quiet stillness that only comes late on Christmas Eve, Ali felt content. She even found herself missing Tommy's parents and little Lulu. She made a mental note to invite them to visit next year.

This year, she had found the balance she had been searching for —the sweet spot between planning and letting go, between tradition and flexibility. She did not need a perfect Christmas. She just needed a joyful one.

Acknowledgements

Writing a book is equal parts caffeine, chaos, and clinging to the belief that somehow it will all come together. I could not have done it without a few amazing people in my corner.

To my mom, Janis, thank you for being my first editor in life and in this book. As a teacher, you proofread every essay and report I wrote in high school and college, so it's only fitting that you were the first to read my very first draft. Your sharp eye helped shape this story in more ways than you know.

To Betsy and Emily, my brave and brilliant friends, thank you for reading the early drafts when plot holes were plentiful, characters were questionable, and punctuation was merely a suggestion. You deserve medals... or at least wine.

To Anne, my book coach and friend, thank you for your insight while answering my endless questions. Our coffee chats and dinners were sanity savers.

And to my two boys, Walker and Blaine, thank you for your patience during the many times I needed to write and rewrite (and rewrite again). You were the first to see the book cover, and I will never forget the way your eyes lit up with pride when you saw my name in print on the cover. That moment will stay with me forever.

I am endlessly grateful for each of you. This book wouldn't exist without your support, love, and willingness to say, "Yes, you're a little crazy—but go for it anyway."

About the Author

KATE HENDRICKSON is a writer and storyteller with a background in journalism and a degree in Mass Communication. Known in her local community for contributing to blogs and magazines, she has always had a passion for writing. She lives in the Florida Panhandle with her husband and their two sons, where she continues to create stories filled with heart, humor, and a touch of holiday magic.

CONNECT WITH KATE

Website: www.kate-hendrickson.com

Instagram: @kwhendrickson

Scan the QR code to stay updated on new releases, book signings, events, and more.